# THE HOUSE THAT HUSTLE BUILT

## PART THREE

Melodrama Publishing
www.MelodramaPubishing.com

This is a work of fiction. All of the characters, organizations, and events portrayed in this novel are either products of the author's imagination or are used fictitiously.

*The House that Hustle Built - Part Three* . Copyright © 2016 by Melodrama Publishing. All rights reserved. No part of this book may be used or reproduced in any manner whatsoever without written permission except in the case of brief quotations embodied in critical articles or reviews. For information, address Melodrama Publishing, P.O. Box 522, Bellport, NY 11713.

www.melodramapublishing.com

Library of Congress Control Number: 2016912059
ISBN-13: 978-1620780671
ISBN-10: 1620780674
First Edition: November 2016

Editor: Brian Sandy
Model Photo: Marion Designs

Printed in Canada

# BOOKS BY

# NISA SANTIAGO

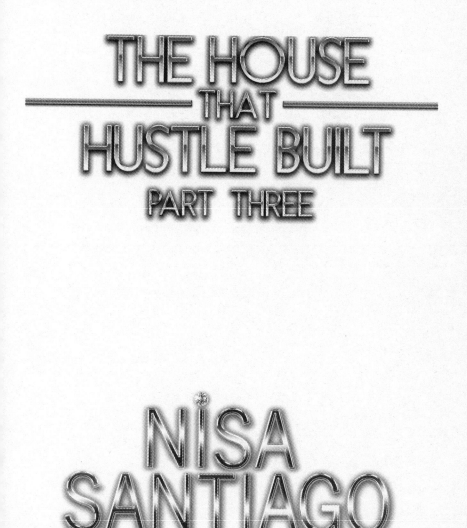

# THE HOUSE THAT HUSTLE BUILT
## PART THREE

# NISA SANTIAGO

# PROLOGUE

Hassan, you got a visitor!" The corrections officer stood there staring at him, waiting for him to move.

Hassan sat for a minute on his small cot, not rushing for anyone. He glanced up at the guard, Officer Clinton. He was a fiery nigga with a badge—a bully with a paycheck. When it came to Hassan, though, Officer Clinton thought twice about being a hard ass. The man was a drug kingpin with a level of clout the corrections officer couldn't even imagine.

Rikers Island was cautious of Hassan, whose fierce, violent reputation preceded him. Though locked down, his influence, money, and power still reigned supreme. In fact, he had authority over the inmates and influence over several guards. An ugly orange jumpsuit and some prison bars didn't change who he was and what he was about. The inmates respected him, and the guards and prison officials were mindful of him.

Sighing, he stood up from his prison bunk and casually walked toward the guard. He had a lot on his mind. The charges pending against him were serious—gun possession and murder. If handled wrong, he could be looking at twenty-five years to life. His lawyers had told him that they were handling his case expeditiously, making strong moves with the prosecutors and the judge.

The two other codefendants weren't talking. No one wanted to cop to the guns and the murders. It was like playing hot-potato.

On the Island all movement was monitored, and every day was the same routine—4 a.m., wake up and a shave; 6 a.m., breakfast; 7 a.m., time outdoors; 11 a.m., lunch; 3 to 5 p.m., mail call and time for napping, reading, and working out; 5 p.m., time in the dayroom where inmates watched TV or played chess or checkers; and after that, dinner and lights out around 9 p.m.

Hassan didn't like routines, and he didn't like being told what to do. He read a lot, worked out, and when he felt the need, held court with some of his soldiers, sometimes in full view of corrections officers.

Today, there was a break in the routine. He had a visitor. Visitors came to see him frequently. He was popular and well known. He was hoping it was Pearla, but she had come a few days earlier. Sometimes she came to see him twice a week. He missed her and thought about her constantly.

After going through the standard procedures before seeing a visitor, including changing into a gray jumpsuit, Hassan walked into the packed visitors' room and searched for the guest of honor. The visiting room was swollen with chit-chat and some laughter between inmates and their loved ones. The guards were strategically placed in different areas of the room watching for anything and everything—contraband, violence, or indecent behavior—and the eye in the sky was recording everything. A female guard directed him toward a nearby table where Bimmy was seated alone, waiting for the boss to arrive.

Bimmy stood up when he saw Hassan walking his way. The two quickly greeted each other with glad hands and a brotherly hug then sat opposite each other, a tiny plastic table between them. The chairs were uncomfortable, but they made do. It was only an hour visit.

"How they treatin' you up in here?" Bimmy asked.

"I'm good. This is just temporary for me, Bimmy; you already know."

Bimmy nodded. "I know."

"Talkin' to my lawyers. They tryin' to execute a plan for my release, but I got something brewing on my own. I can't wait around for these suits to play with my life in their hands."

"Anything I can help out with?"

"I'll let you know."

Hassan looked around the visiting room and noticed other inmates with their girlfriends, wives, sisters, and children. His eyes lingered on one particular male inmate holding hands with his girlfriend. She was pretty, he was handsome. The couple seemed in love. Hassan knew the nigga had sucked another inmate's dick just the night before for some protection from other inmates. Hassan knew many inmates' secrets; most niggas were fraudulent gangsters when inside the visiting room with their families. But after the visit, back inside lockup, they were more bitch than thug—scared niggas who either sold their booty and their souls, or had it taken from them. Hassan was the real thing, and every single inmate in the visiting room knew it. When they saw him, they quickly turned their heads in a different direction, fearing that if they looked at him wrong, there would be problems.

"How's Pearla doing?" Hassan always asked about her.

"You know I always kept it one hundred wit' you, my nigga."

"Yeah, I know. So what bad news you gonna tell me?"

"She ain't right."

"What?"

"I caught that bitch nigga Cash going inside your crib the other night, and he ain't come right back out. He was there for a few hours. I know she fucked him."

Hassan just sat there, staring at Bimmy. Inwardly, he was heartbroken, but there was no way he would express his hurt to Bimmy or anyone else inside the jail. He couldn't get upset and look weak with so many eyes watching.

"You sure it was him?"

"I know it was that faggot muthafucka. I can't mistake him. He was there. In fact, I think he been showing up regularly at Pearla's place since you been incarcerated."

Hassan countered, "It doesn't mean she's fuckin' him."

"What? That bitch nigga is a fuckin' pervert! And you know how Pearla always felt about Cash."

"I know. She promised me that it was over between them."

"Hassan, she broke that promise. She can't be fuckin' trusted."

Hassan knew the truth, but it was hard to accept it. He wasn't a stupid nigga. He knew she'd fucked Cash, but he didn't want to process that image while he was locked up and couldn't do anything about it on his own.

He strongly wanted to believe that it was a mistake. Pearla wouldn't cheat on him. She wouldn't lie to him. She wouldn't go running back to Cash after everything Hassan had done for her. In fact, she was the same girl who had taken a bullet for him. That was love! But what was it about her connection to Cash that she couldn't let go? Did he sex her better? It definitely wasn't his wealth, because Hassan had it all.

Hassan felt he could only get straight answers face to face, looking in her eyes. He wasn't going to react and give Bimmy the orders to murder her.

Speaking softly, Bimmy leaned closer to his boss. "What you want me to do with her?" Both men knew it wasn't safe to relay orders there. Too many ear hustlers were around, from the guards to other nosy muthafuckas.

Hassan sat quietly, brooding. Bimmy was trying to read his boss. If it was him locked up instead of Hassan and he had heard this bad news about April, he would have gone fuckin' berserk. He would have wanted Hassan to cut that bitch's head off and feed it to his pit bull. The thought of April fuckin' the next dude made his stomach queasy. So why was Hassan not affected by the news?

"Yo, just say the word, my nigga, and I can take care of it," Bimmy murmured to him. "It won't even come back on you. If you want it quick or long, it can happen."

Hassan looked at his right hand goon and simply. "Nah, just chill."

"Why?"

"I got this under control, Bimmy. Don't touch her."

"You serious?" Bimmy was dumbfounded by the response.

"Like fuckin' cancer, nigga! I'ma give that bitch enough rope to hang herself."

"That bitch is always swinging, my nigga."

"Then let her swing some more. I got this. I don't want you touchin' one hair on her fuckin' head, Bimmy. That's a fuckin' order."

"Yeah, I got you, boss," Bimmy replied dryly.

Bimmy didn't understand it. What kind of effect did Pearla have on Hassan to make him not react? If it were anyone else, there wouldn't be a doubt or any hesitation; Hassan would have given the word, and Bimmy would have implemented murder immediately. Hassan was playing games.

Hassan noticed Bimmy's sour reaction. "You got a problem with what I said, Bimmy?"

"Nah, no problem."

"Okay, because I don't want her touched at all."

"And if she continues fuckin' with Cash, then what?"

"I'll be home soon, and I'll handle her," Hassan said with conviction.

"In the meantime, she's playing you—fuckin' another nigga in your home, in your bed. How you cool wit' that?"

"Nigga, I don't give a fuck what you think. Don't touch her!"

Bimmy frowned. He felt that the rope was so long, Pearla could have hung herself ten times over. He'd never had a problem expressing himself, but he knew not to cross that line and disrespect his boss.

Hassan couldn't allow his true feelings out, but he couldn't understand why Bimmy was taking this so personally. Pearla wasn't his bitch. "If you're so worried about Cash and my bitch, why is that nigga still breathing?"

"Me and my soldiers been on it, Hassan."

"Maybe not hard enough! Kwan out there too fuckin' up my shit. What the fuck am I paying you for?"

"I never let you down, and I'm not about to start now. Both them niggas will be toe-tagged," Bimmy whispered loudly.

"Just do your fuckin' job, Bimmy!"

At the end of their one-hour visit, the two men gave each other dap and a brotherly hug, and Hassan then pivoted and marched away with the guard's escort.

\*\*\*

Bimmy lingered over his boss's words. He couldn't believe Hassan didn't want to do something about Pearla. She was conniving, and a fuckin' whore. Bimmy felt that bitch had put a spell on Hassan, because he wasn't thinking rationally. That spell needed to be broken somehow. That bitch was making him look weak.

He left the island hoping he would never see the jail as his home. It wasn't a place for men like him. He wasn't scared of jail. He strongly felt that confinement was for animals, not for men.

As he walked toward his car, Bimmy couldn't escape his feelings about Pearla and Cash. Something needed to be done, whether Hassan sanctioned it or not. Hassan was too pussy-struck to see what was clearly happening. That bitch was playing him for a sucker and would certainly cause his downfall. Since Bimmy considered himself a true friend, he wasn't going to allow it to keep happening.

He climbed inside his vehicle and lingered behind the wheel while parked in the jail parking lot. He pulled out his cell phone and dialed area code 678: Decatur, Georgia.

The phone rang several times before a male's voice answered.

"Yo, who dis?"

"Avery, it's your cousin, Bimmy."

"Bimmy, what's good, my nigga? Long time no hurr or see."

"I know. But this ain't a social call, it's something else."

"Speak, my nigga."

"You still runnin' that library?" Bimmy asked.

Avery chuckled. "Hell yeah. What book ya need to read?"

"I got ten large for you to read this bitch a bedtime story."

"Bedtime story, definitely. Ya can check dat shit out right away," he said, knowing a bedtime story meant murder. "Who's da bitch?"

"You don't need to know all that right now. I just need you to show up here, and we'll discuss the details then."

"A'ight, cuz, we in New York," Avery said breathlessly.

Bimmy hung up. He sighed. Going against Hassan's order could mean bringing death upon himself, but he was ready to risk it. By hiring out-of-town killers, Bimmy figured there would be no way Pearla's murder could be connected to him.

# ONE

After receiving the call from his cousin, Avery grinned like a Cheshire cat. He sat on the tattered living room couch, a burning blunt in one hand and a cup of dark alcohol in the other, chillin' with Dalou, his partner in crime.

"Who was dat on the phone that got ya smilin' like that?" Dalou asked.

"That was my cousin from New York. He fixin' to pay us some gwop to do a job for him. Nigga, we 'bout to be in the money."

Dalou smiled. "Word up?"

"Word up."

Both men were short on cash. Hearing about some work in New York made them excited. They didn't care what it was, as long as they got paid.

"Yo, pass the fuckin' blunt, nigga," Dalou said, aching to continue his high.

Avery took a long drag from the blunt, followed by a swallow of liquor, and then handed the blunt to his friend.

That afternoon the two men were in a trap house on the rough side of town. Decatur, Georgia was becoming too small for them. They did it all, from shoplifting, rape, drug dealing, and robbing convenience stores to murder. If it paid, then it was for them, but carjacking and home invasions in Georgia was their bread and butter.

They had no education, no genuine ambition, and were living each day out like it would be their last day on earth. What mattered to them was drugs, drinking, and making a quick buck.

Avery sat slouched on the couch looking like a bum nigga. He was black, skinny, and tall. The white T-shirt he wore was oversized, and his jeans sagged down to his ass crack. He sported short, nappy hair, a gold grill, and had no facial hair.

Dalou was a shorter, skinnier man. His frayed clothes resembled Avery's: oversized white T-shirt, long jean shorts, and Nike sneakers that had seen better days. He too sported a gold grill, short cornrows, and rocked a fuzzy goatee.

"When we leavin' for New York?" Dalou asked.

"Soon."

Dalou nodded.

For Avery, ten thousand dollars was heaven. He couldn't wait to get his hands on that money. It was going to make him feel like a king.

\*\*\*

Before Bimmy's mom passed away the year before, she would always tell him about all the trouble Avery had put their family through with his recklessness. Bimmy's mother always thought her boy was much better, smarter and more successful than his cousin from the South, whereas Avery was nothing but a two-bit common thug with a lengthy rap sheet.

\*\*\*

Avery was such a two-bit thug, he would have done the hit for five hundred dollars. Immediately, he had plans for what he was going to do with all that money. Of course, he would have to split it with Dalou, but that was still five grand in his pockets. It was simple: pack his shit and drive to New York, shoot that bitch, and leave. Afterwards, he would finance a drug package, try to flip his cash and become what he'd always wanted to be—a big-time drug dealer.

"Yo, ya wanna hit da strip club tonight?" Dalou asked him.

"Fuck it, yeah! Get my dick sucked and celebrate our come-up."

"Dis is our time."

"It is, nigga!"

"Ya cousin, he good for it, right?"

"He is. He ain't gonna fuck us."

Both men finished off the blunt and continued to drink. Already, Avery was rolling up another blunt and pouring himself another cup of brown juice. It was definitely time for them to make moves elsewhere.

Avery was ready to prove to his cousin that he was worth every dollar he was being paid. Maybe if they did a good job, Bimmy would permanently put them on the payroll.

# TWO

Hassan sat in Rikers Island's dayroom playing chess with an older inmate named Sammy Grant. Sammy, in his late sixties, was an old-school gangster from Harlem, New York who ran with Frank Lucas and Nicky Barnes back in the day. Sammy was known in the eighties as "the crack king." He used to control so many corners, real estate, and territory between 110th and 135th Streets, they also called him "the black Donald Trump of Harlem."

He had a knack for acquiring properties and knew how to flip them, and he had almost tripled his investments. In his heyday, Sammy was said to be worth close to three hundred million and had as many as a thousand soldiers in his organization. He had close ties to the mob, especially the Gambino crime family. The government finally brought him down in '87. He did twenty years in an upstate prison, and found himself on Rikers because of a parole violation.

The two men played chess together in the dayroom regularly, while other inmates chose to watch television or bullshit around. Hassan wanted to keep his mind sharp, and Sammy helped him with that. They both were skilled at the game, but Sammy had a few more wins over Hassan.

"Your move, Youngblood," Sammy said, snapping Hassan out of his trance.

"My bad, Sammy," Hassan said civilly.

"What's on your mind?"

"Just this case."

"Don't think about it. If you do, it will eat away at you."

"I can't help it."

After the bad news from Bimmy about Pearla, Hassan knew he needed to get out of jail quickly. He couldn't wait around any longer. Every day he became more impatient. His lawyers were working tirelessly on his case, trying to get the judge to allow bail at the next hearing, but his chances were slim because of his reputation, and the bodies on the particular gun he was caught with. But he wasn't alone. His codefendants were indicted too, and they weren't talking either.

Hassan moved his rook to g5, trying to entrap Sammy's knight.

Sammy saw the move three miles ahead. He shook his head, unimpressed. "You're not on your A game today, I see. You gonna allow me to take this game so easily?"

"Shit. I fucked up!"

"Yeah, you did. And it's gonna cost you."

Sammy countered Hassan's move, moving his queen to c3. "Checkmate!" And the game was over.

Hassan leaned back into his chair and sighed.

"Talk to me, young blood. You never been that sloppy." Sammy looked at his young friend. "It's more than just this case that got you looking twisted. I can see it in your eyes."

"Yeah, it is. It's pussy, man."

Sammy chuckled. "A black man's kryptonite."

"Any man's kryptonite," Hassan corrected.

Sammy laughed. "True indeed."

"I need to leave this place, Sammy. I can't think straight. I need to see this bitch and have a word with her face to face."

"What are your lawyers doing for you?"

"Taking too damn long. They pushin' for bail for my next hearing. I can't wait that long."

"We all want out. Sometimes, you just have to play your cards right and know how to work with the hand you've been dealt. I know you're a smart man, Hassan. Just look at the world around you and try to come up with your best conclusion. You're a don, right?"

"You know it," Hassan replied proudly.

"So as dons, we're kings on the chessboard, and what do kings have? Pawns. And what are the pawns' objectives? To protect their king, right? By any means necessary."

Hassan nodded.

Sammy said casually, "Fortunately for you, you have two of your pawns incarcerated in the same house as you."

Hassan knew what Sammy was getting at. He had been playing it cool with his two codefendants, allowing them time to step up and take the rap for the gun. He knew that was asking a lot. But too much time had passed, and he no longer felt merciful.

"Sometimes that pawn may need a little nudging to do what is best for the king."

Hassan nodded. "You right."

Hassan strongly felt that he shouldn't have done one day in jail. His soldiers were supposed to be willing to die for the man that put food in their mouths and fed their families.

Right on cue, one of Hassan's codefendants strolled into the dayroom. Wayne-Oh was a young boy of nineteen and a fierce little nigga trying to hold it down on the Island. Because of Hassan, he was not to be fucked with. He walked around with his head up and shoulders squared, not trying to be some punk in jail. The word was out—the little nigga was connected to Hassan. Hassan fixed his eyes on Wayne-Oh. In a way, he was proud of the nigga yet disappointed.

"There's pawn number one, I see," Sammy said, looking at Wayne-Oh. "You might want to have a chat with him real soon, get him to think differently about the case. Have him see the light."

"I definitely will."

***

The following day at afternoon chow, Hassan sat at the table with a few of his goons, having a regular conversation about pussy and bitches, joking and laughing about some of the best sex they ever had. But this wasn't unusual. Mealtime in Rikers was more like a social gathering for information and gossip. Meanwhile, a few corrections officers patrolled the area, keeping a vigilant eye on certain inmates in the cafeteria.

Hassan was the alpha male in the group; he told the funniest stories and had had sex with some of the baddest bitches, from New York to LA, making him almost a celebrity figure on the Island.

As the group continued to converse, Hassan reflected for a moment. His mind shifted to Pearla. His heart sank when he thought about her infidelity. He had been with hundreds of women, and the majority he didn't give a fuck about. Some bitches in his life were just for bragging rights, some for good sex, and some for business. But for some reason, Pearla was his Achilles' heel. He cared more about her than any other. There was something special about Pearla that didn't make her a dead bitch right away.

Just then Wayne-Oh walked into the cafeteria with another inmate. Hassan had his eyes glued on him. He needed to have another word with the young man. He needed to continue to persuade the young muthafucka. It was now or never.

Hassan excused himself from the table and walked toward Wayne-Oh. A few guards noticed Hassan's hasty movement toward another inmate. Hassan gave a head nod to one of the guards, and he understood.

Hassan walked up to Wayne-Oh, catching him by surprise. "Wayne-Oh, let's talk." Hassan looked at the other inmate Wayne-Oh was with and told him, "Fuck off, nigga!" and the young inmate pivoted and walked away, not wanting any problems.

Hassan threw his arm around Wayne-Oh and said, "Let's walk and talk, nigga." He led him out of the cafeteria, where they had some privacy in a nearby corner. Hassan removed his arm from around Wayne-Oh and looked him in his eyes. "Did you think any further about what you gonna do when you go back into court?"

Wayne-Oh appeared visibly nervous. "Hassan, look, man—"

"What you about to tell me, Wayne-Oh? Some bad news?"

Wayne-Oh sighed. "I've been doin' some thinking, and I had a talk wit' my moms."

"What do your moms have to do with our situation?"

"We just been talk—"

"Nigga, you a grown-ass man, right?"

"Yeah."

"So you don't need your moms to make decisions for you, right?"

Wayne-Oh didn't immediately answer him. "Yo, what you asking me to do, it's crazy! You know how much time I can get if I admit to them charges?"

"Nigga, you think I'm asking you?"

"I showed you respect on them streets, Hassan. I was loyal to you."

"And what? You think that stops in jail? Nigga, you a soldier in them streets and in the jails as well, and when a boss tells you to do something, nigga, you do it!"

"You out your mind, nigga! I eat them charges, and I ain't gonna never see home again. I got a fuckin' son!"

Hassan frowned. "You think you got a choice, huh? You think you got protection in here with your Crip friends? I'm your protection, nigga!"

"Fuck you, Hassan! I'm not fuckin' doin' it!" Wayne-Oh said through clenched teeth. "You ain't askin' for no small favor, nigga. You askin' for my fuckin' life! And I ain't doin' life for nobody!"

"You're not, huh?"

"That ain't my gun, and I ain't body those niggas on it. *You* deal wit' that shit! I wanna get out of here to see my son, and I ain't gonna let you ruin my fuckin' life 'cuz you a fuckin' coward. *You* fucked up, not me."

Hassan kept his cool, though he wanted to smash Wayne-Oh's head through the brick wall. "Fuck it then. Do you, nigga. Have fun," he said calmly, backing away from Wayne-Oh.

After Wayne-Oh stormed away and went back into the cafeteria, Hassan walked into the area shortly after and saw him sitting with a few Crips and chit-chatting. Two Crip gang members looked Hassan's way, and it wasn't a friendly stare. But Hassan kept his cool and went to rejoin his crew at the table.

Several days passed since Hassan had talked with Wayne-Oh, and he didn't make any more attempts to speak to him about the case. Wayne-Oh had his mind made up, and Hassan had to respect that.

***

Wayne-Oh stepped into the jail shower with his necessities this particular evening. Showers were limited, so he planned to be in and out. He wanted to call and talk to his baby mama and his son. One guard was posted outside of the shower, watching the comings and goings of inmates, when Wayne-Oh walked into the open shower, which was already occupied by three other inmates. He proceeded to wash up, while keeping aware of his surroundings.

A minute went by, and then suddenly Wayne-Oh found himself alone. The other inmates had left abruptly, and the guard outside had stepped away for a moment. Out of the blue, Hassan appeared with several OGs behind him. They were armed with some sharp shanks in their hands. They all glared at Wayne-Oh.

Wayne-Oh frowned heavily at Hassan. He already knew what it was. "Fuck you, nigga! You gonna do this to me, like I'm scared."

Hassan casually responded, "You made your choice, nigga, and that choice is gonna cost you your life."

Wayne-Oh was cornered. He tried to stay fierce and tough, but he knew his fate was sealed. A few tears trickled down his cheek as he locked eyes with Hassan, a man he'd once looked up to and taken orders from without any hesitation.

Hassan nodded to the OGs, and they all charged toward Wayne-Oh, who posed in a fighting stance and went swinging for the first man that attempted to penetrate his flesh with a shank. An intense fight ensued with four men, with Hassan watching.

Wayne-Oh, his back against the wall, glared at his attackers. When one rushed his way, he swung wildly and connected his fist with the muthafucka's jaw. But it wasn't enough to deter the men from implementing his murder. The men were too big and too strong. His desperate attempt to shield himself from bodily harm was to no avail. He fought viciously, but one of the men grabbed him from behind in a tight chokehold, and the others repeatedly stabbed him in the chest, torso, and the final strike came to his neck. He collapsed in the shower bleeding profusely, frantically grasping his wounds and choking on his own blood as he lay on the wet, cold tiles.

Hassan looked down at him before exiting the showers. "Stupid muthafucka! You chose death over life in prison. Fuck you!"

# THREE

Pearla walked into her master bedroom wearing a pretty babydoll top and a G-string underneath. Cash was in awe as he lay on her bed. He wanted to devour every inch of her sensual body.

He smiled at her, and she smiled back. "You look good, girl."

"Thank you."

Pearla, her pussy throbbing, hooked her eyes on Cash's naked body. She never got tired of looking at him. From his hard, big, black dick to his tight abs and smooth chest, he was fine. And she could lick the nigga like a lollipop.

Lately, she and Cash had been fucking like rabbits, sometimes rawdogging it. She loved the way his dick felt when bareback inside of her. He knew how to work her pussy, and he wasn't hesitant about coming inside of her. Cash didn't know how to pull out.

But what if she got pregnant? How would she explain that to Hassan? She loved Hassan, but she was still in love with Cash, and when he came around, Hassan was out of her mind.

It was going to be another night of fun and sex. The two barred no holds when it came to pleasing each other. The lights were dim, and the mood was right for some sexual healing, with the two long-stemmed champagne glasses and bottle of Moët on the nightstand.

Cash started to stroke his big dick, teasing Pearla with a nasty show.

"Let's have a drink first," she said.

Pearla wanted to savor the moment with her lover. The sex could wait, but not too long. In the meantime, she wanted to talk and have some foreplay. She wanted to feel his lips against her skin, his tongue between her legs, and to wrap her hand around his hard flesh. She didn't want to be taken for granted. Hassan treated her like a queen, and yet her heart was still with a man who sometimes had the mentality of a child.

Cash looked at Pearla like he would explode if he didn't get any pussy soon. She walked toward the nightstand, and he couldn't take his eyes off her in her sexy lingerie, the translucent fabric accentuating her slim, enticing body.

She picked up the bottle of Moët, which was next to Cash's .45, and filled the two glasses. Cash stood up from the bed, naked and looking like a dog in heat. He would always be her sexy, pretty-boy thug.

As she handed him the champagne glass, he smoothly placed his arm around her waist and pulled her closer and then pressed his lips against hers.

They kissed fervently for a moment.

"Do you love me, Cash?"

"You know I do."

"Say it then."

"What?"

"That you love me. Say it. I need to hear it." Pearla looked intensely at him.

He smiled. "I love you."

"You know how much I'm risking by being with you, especially in this house, the one that Hassan paid for?"

"I don't want to hear about that nigga. He locked up. It's about us."

"I know. It should have always been about us. I don't want to be taken for a fool. I forgive you, but I can't forget, Cash. You hung me out to dry at a time when I really needed you in my life."

"Pearla, I was a fool."

"You damn right, you were!"

"I'm trying to make it up to you."

"It's not just about a big dick and good sex. I want some security, Cash. If Hassan ever found out about us, what do you think he'd do to us?"

"I'm not worried about that fool."

"You never worry about anything."

"Look, baby, I'm a changed man, believe me. I love you, and I will always love you."

Pearla so badly wanted to believe him, but Cash wasn't stable. He never had been. He was in and out of her life continuously, and whenever he came back, she would let him. But things were different now. She was in a relationship with a dangerous man, and Cash was hiding out from his enemies and moving with caution. His paranoia and pistol on her nightstand was evidence of how much shit he was in. Hassan had eyes everywhere. Every move they made to see each other had to be calculated.

Pearla was living her life like it was golden. She had everything she needed: money, fine things, jewelry, and a nice car. She pranced around her home that her man had hustled to build. Whenever she needed anything, she reached out to Hassan, and Bimmy or one of his thugs dropped it off for her. But right now she wasn't in need of anything. She was living the best of both worlds: she had Hassan to support her, and when she needed some dick, she had Cash. It was risky, but the reward was worth the risk.

The sex was calling out to her. They downed their champagne and wrapped themselves into each other's arms again. Cash peeled away the lingerie she wore, and it fell to the floor, leaving Pearla in her G-string. Her hard nipples glistened with perfection. Cash touched her body devotedly, groping her tits and her butt, and they kissed passionately again.

Pearla happily removed the last piece of clothing from her body and straddled Cash's face as he lay back on the bed.

Cash propelled his tongue inside of her and tasted her clit. At the same time he rubbed and massaged her tits.

She arched herself back, grinding her clit against his skilled tongue. Cash was eating her pussy so good, she was ready to come all over his face.

Pearla gyrated against Cash's working mouth and tongue, squeezing and pinching her own nipples. "Ooooh, baby," she moaned. "That feels so good. Yes! Yes! Taste it! Yes!"

Cash was a beast at giving oral pleasure. He made her thighs shake and quiver. The way he cupped her breast and held her firmly, moving his tongue inside of her and focusing mainly on her sensitive clit, had her drowning in pleasure.

Then suddenly, her phone rang. She could feel herself about to come. She ignored the phone call. *Fuck it! They invented voice mail and answering machines for a reason, right?* It felt like time was slowing down. She was ready to squirt her juices all over his face.

As Cash continued with his oral onslaught, Pearla closed her eyes and arched her naked figure even more, gyrating her hips against his face clockwise, both her arms outstretched behind her and her hands flat against the bed, her body feeling like it was about to explode.

Once again, her phone rang. Then it came to her. It was probably Hassan calling. She never ignored his calls. If she didn't pick up, then he would want to know why. Without warning, she jumped off Cash's face and hurried to answer the phone.

Cash looked at Pearla and threw his hands up like, *What the fuck!*

"I need to take this," she said.

Pearla answered the phone, and an operator's voice came on. "This is Rikers Island, and you have a collect call from Hassan. If you accept, please press one, if not, then just hang up."

Pearla quickly accepted his call, knowing it was a risk speaking to him with Cash in the bedroom with her.

Hassan asked, "You busy?"

"No."

"Then why didn't you answer my first call?"

"I didn't hear the phone ring, baby. I'm sorry."

Hassan didn't push the issue. "What you doin', baby? You know I'm thinkin' about you."

"I'm just home alone, doing my hair and relaxing. I'm thinking about you too."

"I miss you."

"I miss you too."

"What you got on for me?"

"I'm naked, lying on my bed."

"Why you naked?"

"I was getting in the shower before bed."

Cash stood naked in the room with a hard dick. He couldn't swallow Pearla, his bitch, having a loving and sexual conversation on the phone with Hassan while he was horny and wanted to fuck. He decided to have some fun. He walked behind her and placed his arms around her waist. He then started to kiss the side of her neck.

Pearla pulled herself away from his hold, spun around, and mouthed, "Are you crazy?"

Cash nodded. He was. He was crazy for her and some pussy.

When Cash reached for her again, she tried to step away from his grasp, but she didn't move fast enough. He grabbed her waist and pushed her down on the bed, and she fell on her back, the phone to her ear.

"I wanna finish what I started," he whispered to her.

Pearla couldn't believe it. Cash was a lunatic. He couldn't wait until she was off the phone. In a strange way, she was turned on by it. It was a pleasure being wanted by two men.

As she continued talking, she felt Cash spreading her legs. She made a feeble attempt to keep them closed, but Cash was relentless, leaving her with no choice but to plant her feet on either side of his shoulders and go with the flow.

"I know, baby. I'm fine. I'm just a bit tired," Pearla said to Hassan. "I wish you were here lying next to me too. I want you so bad. Yes."

Cash ignored their conversation and dove in headfirst, his mouth buried in her pussy.

Pearla squirmed and accidentally moaned. She had to quickly cover her tracks. "That's me moaning for you, baby. You know how you make me feel."

Cash wanted to keep up the fun, proud that he was having sex with Pearla while Hassan was on the phone with her. He started to finger her too, multi-tasking on her pussy.

It was driving Pearla crazy. She moaned again through the phone. She was ready to end her conversation with Hassan, but if she did, that would raise suspicion, if he already wasn't suspicious.

She gyrated her hips against his face, running her hand against his head and ready to dig her nails into his skull. She needed to hold on to something. Cash ate, and ate, and ate, until Pearla was about to come.

Hassan didn't want to hang up, which bothered Pearla. How long could she keep up the charade? All of Cash's attention was focused on her highly sensitive groin area, and every bit of sensation came pouring out of her.

"Did Bimmy come by today?" Hassan asked her.

Pearla had to bite down on her bottom lip abruptly to keep from screaming out in ecstasy. She quickly composed herself and answered, "No, I haven't seen him."

"He gonna come by tomorrow then and drop something off for you."

"Is it cash?" she asked.

"You'll find out."

"What time is he coming by?"

"Just be there when he shows up."

Pearla tried not to concern herself, but it was hard reading Hassan. Sometimes he was just too stoic for her.

She felt another pleasing moan coming on as Cash didn't come up for air, but she managed to stifle it, pressing a pillow against her face.

Hassan said, "I love you, Pearla, and you love me, right?"

Cash swirled his tongue around inside of Pearla, toying with her clit. She closed her eyes, while her man on the other end of the phone waited for a response.

"I love you!" she exclaimed.

She was about to come, and for her not to expose herself, she had to put the phone on mute, so Hassan couldn't hear her. She came so hard and loud, she was squirming all over the bed, and her pussy was squirting like a fountain.

Cash, carrying a look of conceit, removed himself from between her legs and wiped his mouth.

Pearla couldn't keep her phone on mute too long; she quickly composed herself and continued her conversation with Hassan.

Cash wasn't done with her yet, his throbbing dick ready for penetration. Pearla knew the look in his eyes—he was ready to beat her pussy up. She was ready for him. First, she needed to end her conversation with Hassan. She had to be smooth curtailing their talk.

She didn't know how she was going to keep up the act, trying to disguise her pleasurable moment in the bedroom, especially with Cash ready to slide his big dick inside of her. Luckily for her, his phone time ran out, and the phone went completely dead. Pearla was relieved.

Cash grabbed Pearla's legs and pulled her closer his way. With Hassan off the phone, now she could relax and enjoy the dick.

# FOUR

It was five o'clock in the morning and Pearla lay naked in Cash's arms. The time had gotten away from them. After three rounds of deep fucking, they had fallen asleep like babies. Cash was snoring, out cold.

Pearla woke up and immediately removed herself from Cash's arms. She jumped out of bed, panic on her face. What time was it? How long had she been asleep? She was still naked as she ran toward the window and stared outside. It was still dark out. She had no idea what time Bimmy was stopping by. He was unpredictable, and she couldn't risk Cash being there when he came. Sometimes he liked to come inside for unexplained reasons, but Pearla wasn't a fool. She knew he was only checking up on her, spying on her for Hassan. Whatever he saw, he would relay it back to Hassan via phone or during one of his visits to Rikers Island.

"Cash, wake up!" she said, trying to stir him from his sleep. "You gotta go! You need to leave."

Once Cash was asleep, it was hard to wake him up. Pearla nudged him harder and harder. He groaned and slightly moved around on the bed.

She continued to nudge him. "Nigga, you need to wake your ass up! It's almost dawn."

Cash finally opened his eyes, but he didn't rush to get out of bed. In fact, he grabbed Pearla by her arms and tried to pull her back into bed. "C'mon, let's go at it again. Let's go half on a baby."

Pearla pulled away from him. "No more sex! You need to leave!"

"You kickin' me out?"

"Yes!"

"Damn! That's cold. You got what you wanted, so I'm not relevant."

"You already know the deal. You know Hassan always has his peoples coming by to check up on me. I can't risk anyone seeing you here. This isn't just my place."

"What time is it anyway?" He glanced at the clock on the dresser and frowned. "Yo, it's five in the fuckin' morning. You is trippin'? Who gonna come by this damn early?"

"You don't know Hassan."

"Fuck him!"

"I just wanna chill wit' you and enjoy myself."

"We already did enough enjoying ourselves."

"You know you loved it. Don't act like you don't want this dick in you again," Cash said, grabbing his crotch.

Pearla sighed. "Cash, I don't want any drama. I love my life, and I don't want you fuckin' it up for me."

"But you like this dick, though. You wasn't saying that when I was eating you out while you were on the phone wit' that nigga. Most times you the one callin' me to come over. You know what, Pearla? You're a fuckin' hypocrite. I guess now I'm just a booty call, and then you discard me like trash when you're done wit' me."

"You left me and then got wit' some stupid whore!" Pearla countered. "What I'm supposed to do? Keep waiting around for you until you finally get your act together...your fuckin' life right? No, Cash! I'm a bitch that's always gonna do me and look out for me. I've been doin' it before I met you, and I'm gonna continue to do it after you leave."

Cash shouted, "You know what? Fuck it then! I'm out!" He jumped off the bed and quickly reached for his clothes.

"That's what you do best anyway—leave!"

"You told me to fuckin' go!"

"But you don't have to leave here on sour terms," Pearla said.

"I leave the way I wanna fuckin' leave!" Cash scurried around her bedroom collecting his things and getting dressed.

Pearla didn't understand him. He knew the situation—the rules. If he didn't want her to be with anybody else, then he should have stayed with her when it got rough. He chose not to, leaving her vulnerable to Hassan's charm. But there was that child inside of Cash again. He couldn't have his way, so he fussed about it and caught an attitude. Sometimes Pearla wondered what she had seen in him in the first place.

"I'm just telling you we have to be careful," she said politely.

"We *are* being careful."

"We're getting sloppy."

"Whatever!" he spat back.

Completely dressed now, Cash marched out of the bedroom. Pearla followed him. She didn't want him to leave upset.

"Cash," she called out.

"Forget this! Your wish is my command," he mocked.

"You're being fuckin' childish!"

"And you're being ignorant and a stupid bitch!"

"Fuck you, Cash! Get the fuck out my house then!"

"I was already leaving."

"I don't need you!"

"And I don't need you!" He finally turned around to face her. "Go be wit' your prison bitch and catch AIDS when he comes back home."

She slapped him and shouted, "Fuck you!" *Look who's talking,* she thought. Cash was the biggest whore in the city. It was a shock that she hadn't caught anything from him. She got tested regularly, and it always came back negative.

Pearla's eyes were glossy as she stared at Cash. Why couldn't he be better? Why couldn't he change? She was giving him something special even though he didn't deserve it. Her body had always been her temple, but Cash had sometimes treated her like she was a truck stop—a place to rest, wash up and chill, and then head back on the road.

"Yo, I'm fuckin' out," he said. "Don't call me again."

She sighed. "Just leave."

Cash pivoted and walked out the front door. The sun was about to rise. Pearla stared at him walking to his car. She had nothing else to say to him. He was being a fool. He was a risk, but she still loved him.

Cash climbed into his car without looking back at her, and that offended her. He didn't turn around to look at her not once. He started his car and simply drove away.

Pearla slammed the door. She didn't want to think about him, or worry about him. He was never going to change.

# FIVE

Pearla turned on the shower, exhaled and stepped into the steamy, soothing water. For a moment, she let the cascading water beat over her head in steamy rivulets and let the running water massage her muscles. She lowered her head and let her skin become drenched, feeling like she was standing under an everlasting waterfall, her mind swirling with thought after thought.

She had fought all her life to attain the finer things in life. People were always against her. She always had a sheer will to succeed, with or without a man. There was no way she was going back to being poor. The life of luxury she lived now was fabulous. This time she had to be smart and not make the same mistakes she'd made before. The only thing from her past that she allowed into her present was Cash. She had completely abandoned and forgotten about everything and everyone else.

Sometimes, she did feel like a prisoner. Hassan, who was completely crazy about her, had people watching her. She knew it. He was in love with her, but he wasn't a fool. She always had to be careful with the steps she was taking. Sometimes she had to sneak around. He expected her to be faithful to him, but her lust for Cash and her survival was supreme over all.

Whenever she spoke to Hassan, she tried to keep his spirits up by being optimistic about their future together. Despite his battery of high-end lawyers, the gun he was caught with had bodies on it, and there was a possibility that he might not see the light of day. But she continued to support him and be there for him.

With Cash, she was a prisoner of love. No matter what he did, she always allowed him back into her life. Each time he would prove that he was incapable of maintaining stability in a relationship. Sometimes Cash was a lost fool. He was immature and a womanizer; a smart woman would have left the trouble long ago. She had deep-rooted feelings for the nigga. There was that *je ne sais quoi* about him, that inexplicable factor that made him irresistible to her.

Pearla closed her eyes as the hot water soaked into her skin. She leaned against the tiled wall and started to bathe her skin delicately. She enjoyed her showers. They gave her solitude and perseverance, and she came out refreshed and relaxed. She spent a half hour in her steamy bliss, enjoying the water and the Rancé Jasmine Crème Grasse Soap that supposedly had many healing properties. She made sure to cleanse every area of her body. She had Cash all over her skin and needed to get rid of his scent.

Pearla turned off the water and stepped out of the shower. She toweled off, wiped the mist from the mirrors, and stared at her reflection. Such a beauty she was. She did her duties in the bathroom, brushing her teeth, douching and whatnot, and walked out. She had to keep her body and everything else on point. She couldn't slip up. It all mattered, from head to toe. Cash had done some work on her pussy; now it needed to breathe. It was still early in the morning with the sun fresh in the sky, and she had a busy day ahead.

She knotted the towel around her body, walked into her bedroom, and damn near jumped out of her skin with terror when she saw Bimmy sitting on her bed nonchalantly, smoking a cigarette.

"What the fuck, Bimmy!" Pearla shouted. "How the fuck did you get inside my house? You almost gave me a heart attack."

"I knocked and rang the bell a few times, but you didn't answer."

"I was in the shower."

"Well, I made it my business to come inside and make sure you weren't hemmed up in here," he said casually. "Hassan told you I was coming by to drop a package off, didn't he?"

"It's six-thirty in the fuckin' morning."

"And?"

"I'm not even dressed yet." Pearla knotted the towel around her even tighter, making sure none of her goodies were exposed to him.

Bimmy took a drag on his cigarette. "Well, get dressed then." he said.

"Get the fuck out my bedroom!" It was too early for this bullshit.

Bimmy stood up and looked at Pearla. He looked her up and down. He made her very uncomfortable. She couldn't help but wonder what April would think of this. She didn't want any trouble with his baby mama or with Hassan. She thanked God that Cash had left when he did. If not, it would have been hell in her place.

Bimmy slowly walked by her, saying, "I'll be downstairs. Hurry up and get dressed."

"I'm gonna tell Hassan about this."

"He the one that told me if I knock and you don't answer, I got the right to go inside."

"Not to sit in our bedroom and see me in a fuckin' towel."

"Just hurry up and get dressed. I'll be waiting for you downstairs." Bimmy casually walked out of the bedroom, leaving Pearla standing in the middle of the room frustrated and angry.

*The audacity of him.* She slammed her bedroom door shut. She wanted to punch something. She made sure her door was locked before removing the towel. She put on a long T-shirt and a pair of sweatpants and went downstairs to the kitchen, where Bimmy was raiding her fridge, making himself at home, and getting a little too comfortable.

"I hope you plan on making breakfast," she said sarcastically.

He turned around and gave Pearla a chilling look. Before, everything used to be cool with him. He used to treat her like a little sister. She was family. But now Pearla felt some tension with him. He was acting different with her. He was colder. Why? Did he know about Cash? Did he see him come and go? She had no idea what he saw and knew. She kept her cool though. She wasn't about to let this man intimidate her.

"What did Hassan want to leave me?"

Bimmy didn't answer her question right away. He walked by her and went into the living room. On the couch there was a dark plastic bag. It looked heavy. She had no idea what was inside the bag.

Bimmy picked it up and said, "I'm gonna put this inside the safe."

"What safe?" Pearla said. She was confused.

Bimmy walked by her like his name was on the mortgage. He went down into the basement, and Pearla followed him. He turned on the lights and proceeded toward the back of the basement. The area was mostly a storage place for boxes and other junk. Pearla rarely went down there. She was an upstairs girl.

Pearla was still confused. What safe was Bimmy talking about? She'd lived in the house for months and had never come across any safe.

Bimmy went into the laundry room, set the bag on the floor, and removed a few cinder blocks from the wall. The blocks looked heavy, but he was strong. To Pearla's amazement, there was a secret compartment behind the cinder blocks and a safe. How long had it been there? What was inside the safe? The large heavy-duty Sentry safe was fireproof and had a sophisticated dual electronic lock and tubular key.

Bimmy punched in the code, and the safe opened. From where Pearla stood, she couldn't get a good look at the contents, since his frame was blocking her view. He picked up the bag without moving what was inside of it and placed it into the safe, and then he shut it and secured it. He then placed the cinder blocks back where they were, without even breaking a sweat. He turned around and walked Pearla's way.

"You're not gonna tell me what's inside there?"

"It's not your business to know," he replied nonchalantly.

"This is my house."

"Yeah, you keep believin' that," he said, walking out of the room.

Pearla briefly glanced at the area and then followed him. The two went back upstairs. She hated being in the dark.

Bimmy was right about one thing—it was Hassan's house. Though incarcerated, he was still paying the bills, and he still had control of what went on in the streets.

Bimmy looked at her without saying a word, his eyes cold and intimidating. Pearla stared into them and felt an icy chill sweep through her body. There was definitely something going on with him. She couldn't pinpoint what it was, but she couldn't dwell on it.

"How's April?" she decided to ask him.

"She's fine."

"She hasn't called me lately."

"She's been busy," he said dryly.

"Well, tell her to call me."

He nodded. He was about to make his exit. But Pearla couldn't hold her water any longer. She needed to spill. She jumped in front of his path, glared at him and asked, "Do you have a problem wit' me, Bimmy?"

"What?"

"Do you have a fuckin' problem wit' me? Because I'm feelin' some deep hostility between you and me. I'm not feelin' the love, nigga! You come inside my home without me knowing, bring some shit into my house without me knowing what it is. And then you're acting cold toward me, like I did something wrong. What did I do wrong, Bimmy? Huh?" Pearla had her hands on her hips and an attitude on her face.

He stared at her in silence. Then he said, "There's nothing wrong."

"Nigga, you sure? Because the way you're actin', you could have fooled me. What? You think I'm not good for Hassan anymore? You think I'm cheatin' on him?"

"Y'all relationship isn't my business."

"Bullshit! Everything I do, you relay back to Hassan . . . like his bitch."

"Like I said, y'all relationship isn't my business." He pushed his way by her and marched outside.

Pearla sighed heavily. There was something going on. Bimmy knew something but wasn't telling. He had always been the silent and deadly type. If there was a problem, then he took care of that problem. He was the type of nigga who could make a body disappear, or make a statement by executing someone publicly. Pearla was hoping and praying that she didn't become a problem for him and Hassan.

After Bimmy left, Pearla released another long, deep sigh as she closed her door. It was time to pay Hassan another visit. She had to feel him out. She needed more security. She had to remind Hassan that she was his loyal bitch. If she could give him some pussy while he was locked up, then she would. The most she could do for him now was continue to pledge her loyalty to him and assure him she wasn't going anywhere.

# SIX

Cash drove across the Verrazano Bridge into Staten Island nodding to the beat of Jay Z and Drake blaring from his speakers. The sun was still rising, and it was starting to look like a nice day ahead. His mind was on Pearla, as he sang along to the track. Last night was great! The sex was fantastic. She still knew how to make him come hard. Cash's dick got hard just thinking about it.

But she'd pissed him off though. He felt she was putting Hassan before him. He hated that nigga. He knew he'd fucked up, but he was willing to atone for his mistake. Cash felt that Pearla was the only bitch that truly understood him. Why did he let her go? Why did he push that good pussy and beautiful woman into another man's arms? Why hadn't he fought hard enough for her? Why, why, why?

He slid through the toll and continued driving on I-278, traveling deeper into Staten Island. Rush-hour traffic was thickening as the morning developed, and Cash wanted to make it back to his motel room to relax before the good ol' hardworking and taxpaying people flooded the streets and highways of Staten Island.

He made his way south, driving on Hyland Boulevard, and several minutes later, he pulled into the parking lot of the Motel 6 nestled inside the quiet community of Eltingville. The motel was quaint and out of the way, several miles from the bridge, and was the perfect place to hide out. The motel was a temporary residence for him. He paid cash and kept a low profile. He parked his car, and, before making his exit from the vehicle, reached under his seat and removed his pistol. He tucked it into his waistband and made his way toward the motel, moving with steady caution. Cash wasn't taking any chances with his life.

He used his key card to unlock the door and casually walked inside with his pistol in his hand. He flicked on the light. The room was exactly the way he'd left it. There was nothing out of the ordinary. He breathed a sigh of relief and made himself comfortable, double-locking the door and placing his gun on the nightstand near his bed, the safety off. He had more guns in the room and lots of cash. He'd made a lot of money with Kwan and kept the bulk of it in a duffel bag, along with two .9mms and an Uzi.

Staten Island was the last place anyone would find him. The only risk he took was creeping to see Pearla in the middle of the night. But was it worth it? Hassan and Kwan wanted him dead. Both men were deadly and capable of hunting him down. Cash didn't know what to do. His move for now was to keep hiding out, but he couldn't hide forever. There was going to be a day when he would have to confront his foes. He didn't have an army behind him. He just had street smarts, a few guns, and a will to survive by any means necessary. Kwan posed the biggest threat. He was a free man and on the streets looking for Cash. He was a fuckin' lunatic. Cash had seen firsthand how dangerous and deadly Kwan could be.

Hassan was locked up, but there was Bimmy to worry about. The man was a skilled assassin, and he had more bodies to his name than a small cemetery. Bimmy was a calculated killer with people on the streets who could hunt down a fly on a wall. How could Cash go against both men and live? He needed to think. But, today, he wanted to unwind.

He pulled off his shirt, turned on the television, and lit a cigarette. The nicotine pouring into his system was needed. What a night he had! He took a few puffs while sitting on the bed and staring at the television.

The early morning news was on with the traffic report.

Cash had no interest in what they were saying. He finished off his cigarette, removed the remainder of his clothing, and went into the bathroom to shower. He looked reflective in the shower, his head lowered with his arms outstretched and his hands flat against the wall as the water cascaded against his dark brown chiseled flesh.

He thought about his future. He thought about his past. He thought about a lot of things. How would he kill Kwan and Hassan? He thought about Pearla. The sex was great, and she was a good woman, but was it worth putting his life in danger? Although Hassan was locked up, Pearla was still sleeping with the enemy. Mixed emotions poured through him. His life couldn't go on like this forever.

After his shower, Cash toweled off and then lay naked in bed. He lit another cigarette and went over his options. He realized he only had two—go hard or die. He was certain he could kill again. In fact, he felt that he was becoming quite good at it.

# SEVEN

Pearla stepped out of her house in the early morning, looking fresh and clean. The outfit she wore was stunning from head to toe—a pair of tight denim jeans that accentuated her cute, curvy figure, a black top, and a pair of six-inch heels, her sensuous shoulder-length black hair flowing. Her look and clothes were trendy, but still appropriate for her journey to Rikers Island to see Hassan. She climbed into her Benz, started the engine, and briefly checked her makeup in the sun visor before driving off. She felt dreadful going to see Hassan. She didn't know what Bimmy had told him. When Hassan had called the night before, he'd seemed okay, but he was a hard man to read, since he didn't wear his feelings on his sleeve.

Pearla exited Grand Central Parkway and navigated her Benz through the Queens neighborhood as she journeyed closer to the city jail. Feeling apprehensive, she figured listening to Alicia Keys would uplift her mood and give her the nerve to continue on.

It was always a battle going to see Hassan, and the challenge started with finding parking. From the guards to the bleak scenery, it was a dismal and dirty place. Every time, the male guards tried to holler at her, telling her how beautiful she was and asking her why was she wasting her time to see a no-good inmate. The compliments and flirting sometimes were rude and vulgar, and they would carry on from the beginning of her visit until she left. She'd never told Hassan about the harassment from the guards, thinking he already had enough on his plate.

Pearla was able to find parking closer on 77th Street, and she walked the two blocks to catch the Q101 bus going to Rikers Island. As expected, the bus, coming from Queensboro Plaza and headed straight to Rikers, was crowded with mostly women and children.

\*\*\*

The driver steered the bus past the traffic gate, over the Rikers Island Bridge, and onto the island to the central visiting center. Pearla always found it ironic that LaGuardia Airport was next to the jail. She thought the planes climbing steeply into the air from the runway was like a ha-ha to the inmates locked down.

She stepped off the bus with the other passengers and walked toward the visiting center. Most of the ladies on line with her were dressed up as if they were going to a nightclub, some pregnant, others with babies or young children. Pearla thanked God she didn't have any children.

The process for visitors was long and tedious. Before Pearla was able to see her man, she had to go through four different searches and, once again, endure the catcalls from the male guards.

Sitting in the visiting room waiting for Hassan to appear, she minded her business and averted her eyes from people's lingering stare. She was a classy bitch, not like most of the other bitches in the place, looking like they had bullet and stab wounds and bad weaves.

Pearla was a beauty queen, and her man was the boss, controlling the majority of the inmates in the room. That thought put a quick smile on her face. If you were going to fuck someone, then fuck a man of importance. That bitches and inmates knew who she was there to see.

Hassan came walking into the visiting room with a few other inmates all in single file. He moved with authority though he was confined and locked down. He was the first on line. It looked like the inmates coming into the area were following him, although a guard was escorting them.

His gray jumpsuit fit him well. He had been working out and keeping up his appearance.

He smiled Pearla's way. She smiled back. He walked her way, and she stood eagerly to greet him. The two hugged and kissed each other lovingly and then took their seats opposite of each other, still grasping hands across the table.

"I missed you, baby," he announced.

"I missed you too."

So far, he seemed cool and didn't appear to be upset. Did he speak to Bimmy? Was he upset with her but not showing it yet? She didn't want to think the worst.

"Did Bimmy come by and drop off that package?"

"He did. What was in it?"

"It's best that you don't know."

"Why not?"

"It's my business, and the less you know, the more you're protected."

"I didn't know about the safe."

"You weren't supposed to know."

"Do you trust me?" she asked him.

"Why you askin' me that?"

"I just don't like it when Bimmy just comes by unannounced."

"Why? You have somethin' to hide?"

"No! It's just . . . he looks at me differently—like I did something wrong," Pearla said, feeling Hassan out.

"You feel guilty about somethin', Pearla?"

"What do I have to feel guilty about? I have nothing to hide, baby," she said, looking him directly in his eyes and not blinking, her touch assuring him. "I love you. I'm with you until the end."

Hassan squeezed her hand tighter. He didn't want to let her go. He returned her stare, trying to read her soul. But Pearla showed him nothing but passion and concern. Her voice wasn't shaky, and she showed no contrition.

She mentioned to him, "You know, he was sitting in my bedroom the other day and caught me coming out of the shower."

"He saw you naked?" Hassan asked, gritting his teeth.

"No! I had on a towel. But he could have. He just walked into my home without me knowing."

"I'll have a talk with him."

"You need to set some boundaries with him, Hassan. I know you trust him, and he's your friend, but he's starting to overstep. He can't just come in and out of my house whenever he pleases. I'm starting to feel uncomfortable." Pearla pleaded with glossy eyes. She was putting on a great act for her man.

Hassan sighed and repeated, "I'll have a talk with him."

"Please do."

"You're right. There needs to be some boundaries in our home." Hassan leaned closer to her, like he was aching for another kiss. But there was no prolonged affection during visits.

Hassan screwed his face at the other inmates' fleeting looks at his woman. Some niggas were definitely being disrespectful.

"You keepin' strong, and keepin' your head up, baby?" Pearla said.

"I'm maintainin'."

They continued holding hands, all lovey-dovey. Hassan gently stroked the inside of her palm with his fingertips.

Half an hour into the visit, they were laughing and talking, enjoying each other's company, when Pearla decided to spring something on him.

"Baby, I need ten grand," she said.

"Ten grand for what?"

She sighed heavily and looked at her man. "It's my mother. She's about to lose her home."

"You never spoke about your mother before. Why now? I thought you didn't care about that bitch."

"Poochie's still my mother, Hassan. And I still have a heart, and I do love her."

"So now you have a heart for her?"

"She just needs help. She reached out to me the other day. Her man left her and took everything, and—"

"And from my understanding, she was supposed to be forgotten."

"I try, but it's hard to forget when she keeps coming around for help," she lied.

Pearla knew that Hassan knew all about Poochie. Shit, the entire neighborhood knew she was a conniving, loud-mouthed bitch. But Hassan had a soft spot for his fine lady, and whatever Pearla needed, he gave it to her. He knew she'd always tried to be there for Poochie, though she never deserved her daughter's help and love.

"I'll have Bimmy come by and drop it off sometime this week."

Pearla smiled. "Thank you, baby."

\*\*\*

Ten grand was nothing to Hassan. It was punk money. What mattered to him was loyalty and honesty. A month earlier, he had given her twenty grand. She said she needed the cash for an investment. She wanted to better herself and dabble into opening up her own business. Pearla wasn't specific on what kind of business she wanted to start, but her proposition was convincing enough for him to front the cash. A month later, there was nothing. It was all smoke and mirrors.

Their hour-visit went by fast. A female guard approached their table and clearly let it be known, "Time is up!"

Hassan frowned. "I hate this shit. I want more with you."

"I know, baby. I'll be back before week's end."

He nodded.

They both stood up and hugged and kissed passionately for a moment. Their affection had to be brief.

Hassan pulled away from Pearla. He didn't want to get a ticket. "I love you," he told her.

"I love you too."

Hassan made his way back into confinement while Pearla had to sit and wait until the inmates left the area. Jail rules. She released a deep sigh. She hated lying to Hassan, but it had to be done. She needed her reassurance. She had to feel him out, and so far, so good. If he'd suspected something, if Bimmy had said something to him, he would probably have gone berserk and not given her the cash.

# EIGHT

Cash sat in his new ride, a used champagne-colored 2005 Lexus ES with tinted windows. It was a nondescript car and something less than he was used to, but he didn't want to stand out. The Lexus was legit, from the tags to the insurance. He didn't need the headache of driving a stolen car. It was an easy purchase from a dealer in Queens—a friend of his. For eight stacks, his friend effortlessly pushed the paperwork through, gave him temporary dealer tags to drive around in, and he was good to go.

Parked on Dumont Avenue, Cash watched his father in front of the bodega. This time he had moved away from the liquor store, his usual stomping grounds, to the corner bodega and Chinese food takeout spot on Dumont and Rockaway Avenues. It was a busy area with businesses, people, traffic, and the projects across the street.

Cash sat with his pistol on his lap, as he observed his father dancing, joking, and opening up the door to the bodega for approaching customers. Raymond, aka Ray-Ray, was a drunk and a drug user. He was the same joyful, sociable man that Cash had always known. He was full of humor and wise. Though homeless, he always seemed sheltered with happiness.

Cash knew he had to be careful in the area; it was Kwan's stomping ground too. The nigga was a heavyweight in the area, thanks to Cash. The two together, while it lasted, had been unstoppable and thriving in the drug game before it all went to shit. For the wrong reasons, Cash felt.

It had been weeks since he'd last seen his father. It was a risk being there, but he needed to see if his father was doing okay. And he was. Cash lingered on the block and smiled. He missed the lingering conversations with his pops. He missed doing for him, even if it was little things like buying him a cup of coffee or putting money in his pocket when he needed it, though Cash knew it would go to the wrong things. It was hard to see his pops begging, dancing, and doing degrading things just to earn a dollar or two.

Cash lit a cigarette and thought about a life different from his. What if he hadn't been born into poverty? What if his mother was more of a caring, loving mother while he was growing up, and his pops was a hard-working, established man in the community? What if his parents didn't do drugs? What would his life be like? Would he have to steal cars to feed himself? Would he be a whoremonger if his mother wasn't a slut, sucking dick and selling her body in the home while he was young and around to witness it?

Since Cash was a boy, he'd pretty much learned how to take care of himself, knowing the streets. But there was more out there, right? Sometimes he wished he had grown up like the Cosbys.

The truth about him was that he was a womanizing, crack-dealing, murderous car thief with limited friends, if any at all, and a souring reputation. He had done so much hell on earth, it had started to come back on him. Everywhere he went, he carried a gun, sometimes two. Could he continue to live his life in fear and take chances with Pearla, knowing that any moment, death could be right around the corner?

He finished off his Newport and flicked it out of the window. He continued watching his pops from the short distance. He put the car into drive and slowly proceeded closer to his pops. He rolled down the driver's window and hollered, "Hey, Pops, what's good?"

Ray-Ray spun around and saw Cash in the Lexus. He smiled widely, always excited to see his son. "There go my boy! There go my favorite son!"

"Your only son," Cash corrected.

"If I had more than one son, then you would still be my favorite son." Cash laughed.

Ray-Ray said, "I haven't seen you in weeks. You okay?"

"I'm good, Pops. Get inside, let's go for a ride. Let me take you to get something to eat."

Ray-Ray looked reluctant. He was enjoying his day on the corner.

Cash looked around his surroundings, making sure there wasn't any creeping threat. Everything looked okay.

"Why don't you come spend a day on the corner with your old man?"

"I want to take you out to eat, Pops. My treat. C'mon, let's go. You know I'm not taking no for an answer." Cash hurriedly hid the pistol underneath his seat. He didn't want his pops to see the gun and worry about him. He just wanted to spend some quality time with his father.

Ray-Ray stared at his son and relented. "I can't say no to you, Cash." He danced his way toward the car, looking jovial like always. He opened the door and slid inside.

Cash decided to take his father to Olive Garden over at the Gateway Center right off the Belt Parkway. Ray-Ray hadn't been to a nice restaurant in a long while. The two men walked into the restaurant, where the hostess greeted them.

"Two please," Cash said to the petite woman.

Though Cash was well dressed and clean-shaven, his father's clothes were tattered and he smelled of alcohol. The young girl shot a foul look at Ray-Ray.

They followed the girl into the restaurant to their table, a window booth in the corner. It was early afternoon on a weekday, so there wasn't much of a crowd inside. They sat opposite each other, and the first thing Ray-Ray ordered was a drink.

Cash looked at his father and asked, "Pop, you ever thought about leaving town?"

"Leave New York and go where?"

"Anywhere but here."

"Why would you want to leave this city? It has everything we need here. You don't love your home anymore?"

Cash looked reflective. "I just feel like it's time for a change."

"Change? You in trouble, Cash?"

Cash didn't answer his father. He turned away, looking weighty with thought. He trusted Ray-Ray. He could talk to his father about anything, but Cash felt that what he was going through was a little too much for his father to handle.

"Nah, I'm not in any trouble," he lied.

"If you are, you know you can talk to me."

"I know, Pop. That's why I love you."

"I love you too, son."

"Good afternoon, gentlemen. Are y'all ready to order?" the waitress said, standing in front of them with her pad and her pen. She was slim and cute, long hair with a long smile. She was definitely an attractive woman.

Ray-Ray smiled and immediately started to spread his charm. "Damn, you're pretty. I should be buying you lunch," he said to the blushing waitress.

Cash chuckled at his father's words.

"You know, you're too pretty to work," Ray-Ray continued. "I think *America's Top Model* definitely misplaced one of their contestants."

Ray-Ray was on a roll.

The waitress continued to laugh and blush. "You're too much," she said. His tattered appearance didn't matter anymore.

"You don't know the half of it," Cash said.

The two locked eyes. It was clear in her eyes that she found Cash attractive too.

"What will y'all gentlemen be having today?"

"I know what I want, but it might not be on the menu," Ray-Ray said.

"Pop, you need to stop."

"Hey, I'm a man that speaks my mind and goes after what he likes."

"Well, stay focused on the menu."

"I'll try, son. But it's hard to focus when you have a beautiful celebrity standing in front of you. After this lunch, I'm gonna need your autograph, because you're a star in my eyes. Beyoncé don't have shit on you."

Cash said, "Have you ever tried to be normal once?"

"I tried being normal once—worst ten minutes of my entire life."

The waitress started to laugh, and so did Cash. His father was taking his mind off the streets, and away from his troubles. He definitely could count on Ray-Ray to make him laugh, or make him think wisely.

Cash ordered shrimp alfredo. Ray-Ray got grilled chicken flatbread.

"She's pretty, huh?" Ray-Ray said, referring to their waitress.

"Yeah. You already made that clear to her a few times."

"Hey, you have to make it clear; the squeaky chain'll always get the oil."

"You're preaching to the choir, Pops."

Ray-Ray asked, "You have a new girl in your life?"

"Nah, I'm single right now."

"What about that girl you were dating a few months back? What's her name?"

"You mean Pearla?"

"Yeah, I liked her. She was beautiful and smart. How'd ya fuck that up?"

"Just being me, Pop," Cash answered dryly.

"Yeah, I know that feeling. But, hey, they come and go, or we push 'em out with our bullshit. But the good thing about this city, they're everywhere, even serving your meals. You should ask her out."

For the first time in a long time, Cash wasn't thinking with his dick. Normally, he would have been all over the waitress, smooth-talking her, but he had a lot on his mind. It hadn't even come to him to hit on that bitch.

The waitress brought out their food. It all looked delicious. "Enjoy, fellows," she said.

"Oh, we will," Ray-Ray said. "And I love a restaurant with a lovely view," he added, looking her up and down, smiling.

"He doesn't stop, does he?" she said to Cash, smiling.

"He's like the Energizer Bunny—he keeps going and going."

"And where's your energy?" she asked him.

He laughed. Another first, he was speechless. The waitress showed off a welcoming smile his way and walked off.

"I think she likes you," Ray-Ray said.

Cash took his time eating his food. He wasn't in any rush to leave. He was enjoying talking to his father. Sometimes, he felt he would never see the man again. Fond family moments with his parents were so rare, they almost didn't exist at all.

"Pops, you remember that time when you took me fishing in Long Island? I was like ten or eleven."

Ray-Ray went back into his collection of memories, but he couldn't recall that moment. It had been so long ago, and the drugs and alcohol had damn near eaten away all of his brain cells.

"I'm tryin' to remember," he said.

Cash continued on with his story. "Yo, I was so excited. We went to some local bay in the white people area with our fishing poles and bait, and we were out there all day trying to catch something. I was getting impatient, but you told me that if we wait long enough, we'll catch something. I think between us both, we caught three fish."

"I guess we weren't much of fishermen," Ray-Ray said.

"We weren't, but I still had a great time. We listened to music and ate sandwiches. It was just you and me."

"You and me," Ray-Ray uttered.

Cash wanted to remember something joyful, other than reminiscing about sex, whores, stealing cars, and selling drugs. Most of his unforgettable memories were illicit and freakish. He was a boy who had to grow up fast. He'd done a lot, and been through a lot.

"What is it, Cash? You want me to take you fishing again?"

"No, I just wanted to do something special for you."

"This is nice. Thank you."

"It's cool."

As they continued to eat and share a father-and-son moment, the waitress came by their table to check up on them. Ray-Ray flirted with her nonstop, and she subtly flirted with Cash.

When dinner was done, both men stood up from the table. The bill was forty-five dollars. Cash pulled out a wad of cash.

Ray-Ray uttered, "Whoa! Look at Mr. Money here. What you do? Rob a bank?"

"I just came into some money."

"Well, can I come into it too?"

Cash peeled off a hundred-dollar bill and placed it on the table. He and his father started to walk away. They came across the waitress. He said, "Keep the change."

She quickly passed him her number and said, "Call me."

Cash placed the waitress's number into his pocket.

Ray-Ray smiled, proud of his son. "That's my boy."

The men exited the franchise with full bellies after their hearty talk. Cash enjoyed the moment. He stared at his father and said, "We need to be different, Pop. Do something different."

"What you mean? Leave town and start over somewhere else? In a different city?"

"What's wrong wit' that?"

"Look at me, son. I'm too old to start over anywhere. All I know is New York, nothing else. My memories are here, my peoples are here, and some of the best pussy I ever had is here, though that was a hundred years ago. I love this city. I can make my living here. Though it's little, it's still something to me."

"Well, it ain't never too late for change."

"The only change I need right now is to get back on my corner and start entertaining my clientele. I know they're missing me already."

Cash shook his head. He felt his father was being stubborn. But it was his choice. He was seriously thinking about leaving New York for good—to take the money he'd made, find a new town and start over. Too many niggas wanted him dead, and he still didn't know who'd contracted the first hit on him and Pearla. Or who killed his former best friend, Petey Jay. There was too much going on, and too many enemies flowing from different directions. He no longer felt safe anywhere in the city.

Cash and Ray-Ray climbed into the car and drove back to Brownsville. When they arrived back on Dumont Avenue, before Ray-Ray got out the car, Cash slipped him a few hundred-dollar bills and said, "You take good care of yourself, Pops. Be safe out here."

"Same to you, Cash. I love you."

"I love you too, Pops."

Ray-Ray smiled at his son and then stepped out of the car.

Cash lingered in his car for a moment, observing his father, who went to occupy his spot in front of the bodega and carry on with his one-man song and dance. Then he drove away with an uneasy feeling about his father still residing in Brownsville, especially with Kwan in town.

# NINE

Pearla strutted out of her house on a sunny day looking conservative in a well-tailored outfit that flattered her figure but wasn't too revealing or flashy. Her jewelry was modest and tasteful, a necklace of pearl strands and a diamond tennis bracelet, and her long black hair was in a neat bun.

She slid into her sleek Benz, started the engine, and checked her appearance in the sun visor. She was looking flawless. She put the car in drive and sped off. Today she had to tend to some business with the fifteen grand she had on her, plus other valuables. Bimmy had come by the house the other day to drop off the money as Hassan had instructed, and he didn't look too happy about it.

Pearla hit the freeway and headed toward the city, to the bank, one of her many stops for the day. Lower Manhattan was congested with daytime traffic and frantic with people. The towering skyscrapers were an indication of wealth and power. It was a town made of money and partnerships. Manhattan, especially Lower Manhattan, was an iconic place for her. She loved money and success.

She parked her Benz inside one of the pricey garages that dotted the area and walked toward the National Savings Bank on Broadway in her Louboutin shoes to meet with Ralph Prestano, one of the bank managers. He was a tall, lean white man with short, curly black hair and a friendly personality. The Harvard graduate was dressed nicely in a three-piece suit.

The moment he spotted Pearla walking through the front doors, he made it his personal business to go over and greet her. "Pearla, it's always good to see you," he said.

"Hey, Ralph."

The two shook hands.

"What brings you back so soon? Another deposit?"

"Of course. A girl always has to put something toward her future." She pointed toward the small black satchel she was carrying.

"I understand. Follow me."

He guided her toward the rear of the bank, and they walked into the vault, with its many safety deposit boxes. She signed some paperwork, presenting the proper signature needed and presented her key. Ralph presented his key too. He went to two boxes that she had. He placed his key into the lock and turned, partially opening the box.

Pearla followed suit, inserting her key into the boxes and opening them completely, gaining access to the goodies inside them both.

Ralph smiled. "I'll let you carry on with your business alone." He walked out of the bank vault, giving Pearla some privacy.

Pearla removed the long rectangular containers, set them on a nearby table, and opened them both. Inside one was one hundred and fifty thousand dollars in cash. The other had jewelry, important documents, her passport, and pictures of her and Cash. The jewelry in the box was worth half a million alone. Her whole life was in it. She wasn't taking any chances. If anything were to happen, she would have a lot to fall back on. Most of the money she'd saved from scams she'd implemented; the rest was from Hassan, who had been very generous to her over the months.

She removed a ten-thousand-dollar stack and placed it into the safety deposit box with the rest of the loot. She took a few more pieces of jewelry from the satchel and put them in the second box with the rest. It was a pretty thing to see. She smiled. She had enough saved for a rainy day.

She spent less than fifteen minutes inside the bank vault. Some of her time was spent looking at pictures of her and Cash during happier times when they were together. One picture was of them at Coney Island, another was of them hugged up on the block, one was in a nice restaurant, and the others were various photos of them together throughout the city.

Pearla secured everything in the boxes and placed them back into their locations. She and the manager locked them with their keys and walked out of the vault.

"Was everything satisfactory?" he asked her.

"Yes, it was."

He smiled. It was clear that he liked her. "Next time then," he said.

"Next time." Pearla turned and strutted out of the bank, leaving Ralph's eyes lingering on her backside.

She jumped into her Benz and sped to the high-end stores on Fifth Avenue. Fifth Avenue was the Mecca of shopping. From block to block, north to south, it was a shopper's paradise. Over the years, she'd tried to shop in every last one of them. She had a thirst for fine fashion and knack for style.

She climbed out of her Benz clutching her Fendi purse in one hand and a shopping bag in the other. She went into the Chanel store. They had it all: luxury jackets, apparel and more. She walked into the store with some of their items.

"Hello, can I help you?" one of the female workers asked.

"Yes, I'm simply here to return some items," she said.

"Oh, I'm sad to hear that. What items do you want to return? And why?"

"You see, there's been a little mix-up between my husband and me. It recently was my birthday, and though I like to treat myself, my husband went and treated me to the same thing I recently bought. He definitely knows my style." Pearla removed the pumpkin-colored jacket and a

Chanel purse and placed them on the counter. The two items combined were worth $15,000.

The lady inspected the items. The price tags were still on both items and they were untouched, brand-new still. "Well, happy belated birthday, and I assure you, we'll get you taken care of."

Pearla smiled. She didn't need the extra money, but she planned on returning everything that Hassan had purchased for her—well, mostly everything. She had a receipt for everything. Pearla had always been a meticulous girl. She knew how to work the system. Shoplifting was once her forte.

The young girl rang up the items she was returning. She then looked at Pearla and said, "You know, we can offer you store credit, if it's something you're interested in."

"No, thank you. I'm fine with just receiving my refund."

The girl smiled to cover her annoyance and continued with the process. Department and boutique stores hated returns. They almost treated you like you stole it when you asked for your money back. Pearla didn't care. She just wanted the extra cash. She had tons of clothing, purses and jewelry in her closet. She had more clothes and shoes in her closet than she could wear. She was returning a few things, and yet her walk-in closet was still jam-packed with stuff. If Hassan ever came home, he wouldn't even notice.

After confirming the refund with her manager, the girl pulled out a stack of cash and started to count out hundreds and fifties in front of Pearla, who placed the money in her purse, smiled at the ladies, pivoted, and walked out of the store a proud bitch.

She climbed back into her Benz and headed to her next destination. The exclusive nail salon on West 58th, two blocks away from Central Park, was where the wealthy and privileged went to get the best manicures and pedicures in town. Lady celebrities were known to frequent the establishment. It was where the Koreans could draw some of the most intricate designs on finger- and toenails. Their massages were soothing and treasured, and they served lattes, sushi, wine, and other rich delicacies to their customers. It all came with a price, though.

Pearla pranced into the salon wearing her oversized Gucci shades. Usually, it was appointment-only, but she was a regular and a great tipper. Once she walked into the place, she was like Norm on *Cheers*: everyone knew her name. The workers wanted her, because she was known to hand out fifty- to hundred-dollar tips for some of their finest designs.

She was immediately escorted to the leather spa massage chair, one of the best the place had to offer. The place was packed with affluent females enjoying treatment from top to bottom. A regular, hardworking woman would have to put up her entire paycheck for a pedicure alone.

"What ya want today, Pearla?" the Korean employee asked her.

"I just want something simple but classy."

The pedicurist was ready to clean, shape, and beautify her toenails, and then her fingernails.

Pearla sipped on an espresso, enjoying the benefits of the spa chair while her feet were being cleaned. She couldn't imagine ever giving all of this up. Though she had to fuck a big-time drug dealer to keep it, it was worth it. Who wanted to live poor? Not her.

She closed her eyes and enjoyed the fruits of her illegal labor. She did it all, shoplifting and murder, scamming and fraud, even sexing the right nigga to have a lavish lifestyle. No regrets! This was it, how a bitch like her was supposed to live. She was having great sex, but not with her man.

Pearla knew from experience that one day, it can all come to an end, crashing down suddenly like a plane out of a sky. So she was saving and planning, and when push came to shove, she would have enough money to fall back on and rebuild. Maybe leave New York and start somewhere else.

As the pedicurist worked on her toes, she pulled out her smartphone and stared at the screen. She had no missed calls and no unread text messages. She thought about Cash. He hadn't called. Of course he hadn't. He was too arrogant to call her. But she thought about him frequently. More than she thought about Hassan.

She wondered how Cash was doing. Was he okay? Why didn't he reach out to her? Yes, they had a little spat, but they always had a spat here and there. It had been a week, and she was starting to worry about him. She knew the predicament he was in, fearing for his life, not just with Hassan, but with Kwan and other enemies lurking.

Pearla scrolled down to his number and stared at it. She was tempted to call him, but she stopped her action. *No, I'm not going to call him. He needs to call me,* she said to herself. But her pussy was throbbing and talking loudly. With Hassan locked away, Cash was the only man she wanted to come over and play.

Instead, she decided to scroll to another number and call it. She needed a distraction from Cash. She pressed the call button, placed the smartphone to her ear and heard it ring several times before April answered.

"Hey, girl, what you doin'? It's been a while," Pearla said.

"Hey, Pearla," April replied dryly. "What's up? And why you callin'?"

Pearla was somewhat taken aback by the antagonism from April. She had always been blunt, though. She ignored it. "I haven't heard from you in a while. I was just thinking about you. Everything's okay?"

"Everything's fine."

"That's cool. Hey, what are you doing later on? I was thinking, let's meet up and hang out, maybe get some drinks and have girl talk."

"To be honest, Pearla, I don't have the time right now."

"Why not?"

April replied, "I just don't. What? You my parole officer now?"

"I was just thinking about you."

"Well, I got things to do. Me and Bimmy been goin' through some rocky shit."

"I'm sorry to hear that, April. You know I'm around to help, or if you need to talk to someone."

"Well, I'm a big girl. You don't need to hold my hand whenever shit ain't right wit' my man."

"I know. I was just trying to help. I wanted to treat you to a spa day, or lunch, help you get your mind away from drama."

"Ain't no drama in my house, boo-boo, just some regular couple beef. And I'm handling my shit," April said sharply.

Pearla couldn't break through to April. April had been acting really funny lately, cold and distant, just like Bimmy.

"Okay, well, I'm gonna let you go. You got my number. If you need anything, just call me."

"Bye!" April said, being short.

Pearla sighed and decided to shrug it off. *Don't let that bitch ruin your day*, she told herself.

She went on to enjoy her pedicure. Kim was doing magic with her feet and her toes. Pearla leaned back, and the spa chair was also working magic on her body. It was hitting her nooks and crannies nicely.

Once again, Cash came into her head. The recent night with him was just too memorable to put out of her mind. Thinking about it had her pussy tingling.

*Don't call that nigga*, she reminded herself. *He ain't worth it. He didn't call you yet.*

But it was a losing battle to not think about him. She pulled out her smartphone and once again scrolled down to his number. She stared at it. Her body and her pussy was trying to speak for her. Her common sense was steadily being replaced by lust. She exhaled. She wanted to fight the urge. *Don't call him! He's a big risk.*

She decided to text him: HEY, WHAT U DOIN'?

She sat back and waited for him to respond.

An hour went by, and still no response. Pearla frowned. The thought of Cash not texting her back was souring her mood. *Why is he ignoring me?* she thought. *He gotta be fuckin' the next bitch. You stupid for letting him inside of you. Is he worth it?* She was thinking about all kinds of craziness. The more time that passed with her smartphone idling, the sourer she became.

"I don't know why I keep playing myself," she said out loud to herself. She released a deep, irate sigh and decided to just enjoy her day at the spa and try not to think about him. But the nigga was so deeply rooted into her soul, body, and mind, she almost felt breathless without him around.

After two hours in the high-end nail salon, Pearla's feet and nails were looking like a million bucks. Kim did her thing. Pearla was pleased with the design on her tips—a multi-composition of colorful flowers and roses on each nail, with matching toes. It was impressive. *Let the hate start.* Pearla smirked. The price tag was four hundred dollars, and she tipped Kim a C-note.

The minute she walked out of the nail salon, her smartphone chimed. She removed it from her purse and saw a text from Cash. She smiled and quickly read it.

I'M CHILLIN', WHY?

Pearla immediately texted him back: I'M THINKIN' BOUT U. I WANT 2 SEE U. ☺

WHEN?

2DAY?

OKAY, I'LL CALL U.

DO THAT. I MISS YOU. DO U MISS ME?

He texted back: U KNOW I DO

Another ☺ from her.

BUT I'M NOT GOIN' BACK THERE AGAIN, 2 YA PLACE. 2
RISKY.

I UNDERSTAND. MEET ME THEN. OR I CAN CUM SEE U.

DAT CAN WORK. TALK 2 U LATER. BUSY RIGHT NOW.

She replied: BYE BABY. CAN'T WAIT.

Pearla was smiling from ear to ear. She walked back to her car in a
better mood. It took him long enough, but he finally hit her back. Like
always, she had reached out to him when he was the spoiled brat who had
started their argument. But that dick was worth it, and she loved Cash.

She climbed into her Benz, once again exhaled, and drove off. She was
looking fantastic from head to toe, and she couldn't wait until her insides
below felt the same way she was feeling, and only Cash was capable of
making that happen. She was hoping he didn't wait too long to call her.
Her body felt like it was about to explode.

# TEN

*Decatur, Georgia*

An old, brown Dodge Caravan came to a stop in front of one of the many big houses in the affluent neighborhood. Known for its spacious single-family homes with manicured lawns from block to block, Glennwood Estates was a wealthy enclave within Decatur. It was early afternoon, and the area was quiet.

Avery and Dalou sat parked outside a two-story brick home with a two-car garage at the end of a hilly driveway. They were scoping out the place, planning on making their move. The afternoon hour most likely indicated that the residents of the home were either at work or running errands for the day. The place looked quiet and empty, with no cars parked in the driveway or out front, and the block was thin with cars and people.

Avery took a drag from the Newport burning between his lips, the nicotine a substitute for a blunt. They wanted to get high, but first they needed to focus on the task at hand.

"What you think?" Avery asked Dalou.

"Looks perfect."

"You wanna check?"

"Nah," Dalou said. "It's ya turn."

"No, it's ya turn. I went last time."

"No, stupid, it was me. I'm always checkin'."

"Bullshit!"

"You da bullshit!"

They started to bicker in the front seat of the caravan. A crowbar, gloves, masks, and other tools used for burglary sat on the rear seat. Avery took a few more pulls and shared the cigarette with Dalou. Both men stared at the front entrance to the house.

Dalou said, "One of us needs to make sure."

"Rock, paper, scissors," Avery suggested.

"Fine!"

"Rock, paper, scissors says shoot!" Avery exclaimed.

Both men shook their fists in the air and simultaneously formed one of three shapes with their outstretched hand. Both men formed rock.

"Damn, you cheatin'!" Avery hollered.

"Nigga, you cheatin'. Again," Dalou said.

"Rock, paper, scissors says shoot!"

Avery formed paper, and Dalou formed a rock. Avery laughed and said, "Ha, paper wraps rock. You check."

Dalou said, "You fuckin' cheater!"

"What am I? A mind-reader?"

Dalou sighed.

"Nigga, we need dis money. How else we gon' get to New York?" Avery asked.

"Yeah, whatever!"

Dalou climbed out of the Caravan. He took a quick glance at his surroundings and marched toward the front door. He went up the concrete steps and stood between the thick shrubs, which concealed his identity from the neighbors in case they were peeking from their windows.

He took a deep breath and knocked on the front door. What would he say just in case someone answered? He came up blank. He knocked again, but no one came to the door. It was the perfect time. Dalou turned to face

Avery and gave him the thumbs-up.

Avery smiled. He collected their tools from the backseat and hurried toward the house. Both men hurried toward the backyard, scaling a short white fence and moving toward the back door. No dogs. Perfect! The backyard was cluttered with trees and bushes, providing the perfect cover for them as they implemented their break-in.

They went onto the short patio with its glass sliding doors. Avery and Dalou had committed the act plenty of times and it had become routine. Avery pulled out the crowbar and went to work on the doors, while Dalou stood as lookout. Avery quickly forced the glass doors open, and they hurried inside. The first thing they looked for was an alarm panel. Lucky for them, there was none. That meant no police.

"Let's hurry up and do this. You take upstairs, I'll check down hurr," Avery said.

Dalou nodded.

Both men wore gloves and carried a knapsack. Dalou rushed upstairs. The house was nicely furnished. There was a large flat-screen in the living room, but it was too big to carry, and an item like that created too much attention if they were to move it out the front door. They were going for the little things of value: jewelry, cash, watches, anything they could put into their knapsacks.

Dalou went straight for the master bedroom. He turned over the mattress and looked under the bed. He went into the walk-in closet and found jewelry and cash, plus some credit cards. Everything went into his bag. Then he went into the bathroom. He opened the medicine cabinets and looked for prescription pills, and hit payday. Pills were easy money.

Avery searched around downstairs. He tore the kitchen and living room apart looking for electronics, credit cards, and personal information. He placed an X-Box and a few games into his knapsack. He found a cell phone. Then he removed some china and silverware from the cabinet.

Dalou came downstairs and smiled at Avery. "Yo, it was definitely payday upstairs," he said.

After they gathered everything they needed, they rushed outside via the back door and rushed toward their vehicle. Avery got behind the wheel, and he put the van into drive and was ghost. It took them no less than twelve minutes to get in and out of the home. It was an easy score.

***

After fencing everything they stole from the Glennwood Estates home, they received five grand for everything. They were expecting more, but their fence reminded them that stolen goods were harder and riskier to move, although it was valuable stuff. Five grand was better than nothing. They had more than enough to fund their trip to New York to carry out their contract.

"Ya wanna hit da strip club tonight?" Dalou asked. "Shit, we got more than enough for New York."

"Yeah, that sounds like a plan."

The strip clubs in Atlanta were some of their favorite places to be, where they could enjoy the scenery and overindulge in liquor and beer. Onyx on Cheshire Bridge Road was three hundred and sixty degrees of nudity, and girls with the most acrobatic pole skills.

Avery and Dalou had front row seats to all the flesh they desired. Having twenty-five hundred a piece, they were ready to tip the girls handsomely. Girls, girls, girls—they were everywhere in the energetic club, the front, in back, above and even below. Women in all stages of expression in every position, and with every body part moving seemingly independently of the rest. The music was loud and upbeat, and the place was swarming with men.

Avery clutched fistfuls of singles and fives. He was downing Patrón like it was water and lusting after every dancer that worked the stage, his eyes transfixed on their voluptuous bodies as they twerked perfectly. Dalou was becoming a drunken mess himself, tossing money at the girls and shouting obscenities.

Now that they had money to flaunt and were making it rain on the stage, both men felt they could do whatever they wanted inside the club.

One stripper had Avery's undivided attention. Strawberry Alice was a dynamite woman with a mocha complexion and Coke-bottle shape. Everything on her was flawless. She was one of the classiest girls in the place, with long hair and no stretch marks.

Avery was in love with her. He threw a hundred dollars in singles her way, and the money floated everywhere in a cloud of green. He hollered her way. "Yo, beautiful, won't ya come ride dis dick tonight?"

She ignored him and continued dancing.

It was mostly well-dressed clientele inside of Onyx. Avery and Dalou were the oddballs. Avery threw more money her way and downed his umpteenth shot of tequila.

"I think she likes you," Dalou said. "Look how she's shakin' her ass for ya." He laughed.

The two men had always been local troublemakers. They started fights and sometimes performed robberies on drunken patrons leaving the club. Though they were never caught doing the crime, everyone knew it was them. They always reeked of foul play. Their reputations were tarnished from club to club. The bouncers were watching them, already on standby for the inevitable to happen.

"Yo, bitch, why you dissin' me?" Avery shouted. "C'mere!"

She turned her nose up at him. Instead, she gave her naked time to the more respectable gentlemen inside the club. It was mostly well-dressed clientele inside of Onyx. Avery and Dalou were the oddballs.

"Damn, Avery! Why ya girlfriend rejectin' you, huh? Ain't you spent enough on that bitch for a dick suck?" Dalou laughed again.

"I know, right?"

Avery stood up and tossed more money her way. He shouted, "Hey bitch, my money ain't good enough in dis club? Ya not tryin' to fuck wit' me, huh?"

"She ain't, nigga."

Out of nowhere, Avery rushed onto the stage and grabbed Strawberry Alice by her wrist, jerking her in his direction. She stumbled in her clear stilettos and screamed, leaving the regulars in shock.

Several bouncers immediately hurried to the stage. Before Avery could assault her or touch her inappropriately, they grabbed his collar and more of him, and tried to remove him from the stage.

Avery wasn't having it. He jerked free from their grasp, spinning around and shouting, "Get da fuck off me!"

"You need to leave!" one of the bouncers told him.

"Fuck you!" Avery cursed. But it was definitely the alcohol talking.

They rushed at him, and he swung wildly at them, and a fight ensued on the stage. There was a heated tussle between Avery and three bouncers. He wasn't going down or leaving without a fight.

Dalou quickly hurried to help his friend. He leaped onto the stage like he was a superhero and went charging for the nearest bouncer, punching one in the back of his head, and shouting, "Get off my nigga!"

The girls ran for cover, and the patrons were moving in a different direction.

All of a sudden, bottles and glasses were being broken. A chair was thrown, and more people got into the intense brawl, Avery and Dalou right in the middle of the chaos.

Heads started to bang, blood spewed from mouths, and fists went colliding with faces and body parts. Avery was strong and vicious. Though he was outnumbered, he was fierce with his hands. The tequila made him feel invincible. Dalou was ready to shoot someone, but no guns were allowed inside the club.

Soon, both men were on the floor and being beaten viciously, boots and fists went crashing into their bodies. Dalou had to place himself into the fetal position to protect his vitals. And Avery had blood oozing from his mouth, his knuckles bruised from punching muthafuckas left and right.

The bouncers carried them out like trash, after picking them up from the floor like rag dolls.

Avery screamed madly "Yo, get the fuck off me! Get the fuck off me!" He squirmed and fought back relentlessly, trying to free himself from their grasps. But to no avail.

Dalou was the easier of the two to throw out of the club, since he was shorter and skinnier than his friend.

They both were fighting a losing battle. Avery and Dalou were violently ejected from Club Onyx and found themselves in the hands of Atlanta PD. They were immediately arrested and taken into custody. It looked like their trip to New York was about to be put on hold.

# ELEVEN

Kwan loaded a full clip into the Desert Eagle .50-cal., a sleek, powerful semi-automatic handgun. The weapon had become an icon everywhere in the world with its triangular barrel and gaping muzzle. In the wrong hands, it became a murderous weapon, able to kill a man easily. He cocked it back. He held the weapon in his hand like it was his own son, the way he admired it. Tonight he was ready to put it to good use.

He rode shotgun in the moving Tahoe truck. He was among other killers: T-Mack, Holland, and Ricky, who were all armed, dangerous, and ready to execute some payback. Brooklyn, especially Brownsville, was their territory. They were still at war with Hassan and his organization. Though the man was locked up, he was still a dominant force in the borough, among other areas. Bimmy was a threat to them. He was just as deadly, maybe even deadlier. There was a major contract out for Kwan and Cash. Both sides were gunning for each other, desperate to spill blood like they were gladiators in a Roman arena.

Kwan took a pull from the blunt in his hand and inhaled the lovely Kush. The high was motivating. He had the urge for chaos. He had a yearning to wear the crown. He had established himself with a new drug connect, some Colombians from Washington Heights, and he was about to make the city his playground. He felt untouchable like a demon—a hell spawn ready to spit fire and burn down his enemies.

He took one more pull from the blunt and handed it off to the driver, T-Mack. The weed smoke lingered inside of the car. Kwan peered out of the window, focused on the people and the streets. His streets. He had twenty kilos of potent heroin (black gold) ready to move into the area, but some of it was Hassan's turf. The beef between the crews wasn't just personal, it was business too.

Kwan said to his crew, "Look, we don't hesitate. We go in here, kill these niggas—especially Bimmy—make a statement, and we out."

Each man nodded as T-Mack neared the Tahoe to their destination, the Brownsville Projects on Livonia Avenue. Everyone had killed before. It wasn't brand-new to them. So Kwan felt comfortable with his men.

Some of Bimmy's men had set up shop in an apartment building and made it their business to distribute heroin into the community. They were making their presence known in a big way. When a few residents warned them about Kwan, they insulted his name and wrote off the warning as an empty threat. They were connected to Hassan, and they took orders from Bimmy, no one else. In their eyes, Kwan was nobody, a fledgling hustler. But Kwan was ready to prove them wrong.

It was late in the evening on a cool, sunny day. Lots of folks were coming home from work, and kids from school. The corner of Rockaway and Livonia was bustling with pedestrians, residents coming and going, and vehicular traffic. Numerous shops lined the avenue, the tiny strip mall nestled inside.

"Yo, slow down, nigga!" Kwan instructed.

The Tahoe slowed down at the corner and made a left.

Kwan was keeping a keen eye out for any nigga that wasn't part of his crew. He had eyes and ears everywhere on the streets. He already knew the building and the apartment number his enemies were occupying.

"Where they at?" Holland asked.

Kwan nodded to the third building on the avenue. "They up in there—Apartment 10F."

"Let's do this then, nigga," Holland said, itching to shoot his gun.

"You think they ain't got guns and soldiers too? We think rational on these muthafuckas—do it right. I don't want any mistakes," Kwan said.

"How you wanna do it then?"

Kwan went into thinking mode. He sat quietly in the front seat, trying to find a way to smoke these niggas out.

Kwan's intuition was screaming at him. Something didn't feel right. The information he received, could it be that easy, so simple? Before, Bimmy's crew had never made it so easy for them. All of their safe houses and trap houses had been fortified with lookouts everywhere. And Bimmy hardly made himself so vulnerable in Brooklyn, or anywhere else. Why now? Why was he in the housing project on this particular day?

Kwan though maybe his mole Tony had given him bad information, playing both sides of the fence. As far as he knew, it could be a setup.

The men inside apartment 10F weren't some random street thugs encroaching on a street corner selling ten-dollar crack vials and packing one or two pistols. Nah, they were organized and well-armed. They were part of a well-oiled machine. They might have eyes on the rooftop looking out for law enforcement and rival crews looking to invade suddenly.

"Yo, Kwan, how you wanna do this?" Holland asked again.

"I'm thinkin', nigga!"

"Nigga, what the fuck is the problem kickin' in the fuckin' door and just sprayin' the whole fuckin' apartment?" Ricky said. "I'm ready to take these niggas out and eat!"

"Because, nigga, we don't know what kind of guns they got up in that bitch. You think they gonna have more than ten ki's inside and simply carry pistols and revolvers? And what if Bimmy's inside too? Think, nigga!"

"So we just gonna sit here lookin' stupid, like some scared bitches?"

T-Mack said.

"Nigga, what's up?" Holland asked, becoming impatient.

"Something ain't right," Kwan let them know.

"What the fuck you talkin' 'bout? You got the info, nigga, and you ain't gonna use it?"

"I'm talkin' about over a month of tryin' to find this nigga, and it's gonna be this easy? This nigga Bimmy ain't stupid."

"Yo, we can wait for him to leave and then push that nigga's wig back, blow his fuckin' brains out for everybody to see," Ricky said. "I don't give a fuck."

They could. But who was watching them? Who was waiting for them to strike and fuck up? Was Bimmy even in the building? Was apartment 10F reliable information? Kwan was hunting for him and vice versa—Bimmy was hunting for him.

Kwan said, "Y'all niggas chill for a minute; let me see what's up." He concealed the .50-cal. on his person, pulled up his hoodie, and got out of the Tahoe. He tried to look as inconspicuous as possible, pulling his ball cap low over his eyes.

He walked toward the building, leaving his team of killers seated inside the truck. Every step Kwan took was calculated. His eyes darted everywhere, and he read everybody in passing, wondering if they were friend or foe. He kept his reach near his concealed .50 cal. Kwan tried to stay calm as possible, though he was on high alert. He wasn't dealing with an amateur.

"Yo, shorty, c'mere," he called over a young kid who looked to be in his early teens.

The kid hurried toward Kwan. "What's up?"

"What's ya name, little nigga?" Kwan asked.

"Michael."

"How old are you, little nigga?"

"Twelve."

"I need you to do me a favor, Michael." Kwan reached into his pocket and pulled out a wad of hundred-dollar bills.

Michael's eyes lit up brightly.

He peeled off a C-note and put it in the kid's hand. "This ya building?"

Michael nodded.

"What floor you live on?"

"Eight."

"Okay, I need for you to knock on 10F for me. Pretend you lookin' for your moms or something, and then come back down and tell me who comes to the door and what you see."

It was a simple task in the kid's eyes. For a hundred dollars he was willing to do whatever he was told.

Michael went running into the building, while Kwan stayed behind in the lobby, simultaneously watching the door, the elevators, and the stairway, his gun close and cocked back.

Several minutes passed and still, no Michael. Kwan was becoming impatient. Was it a mistake to pay the little nigga before he completed his mission? Or did he put the little nigga into a situation where he bit off more than he could chew? Either way, it wasn't looking good.

Then out of the blue, the elevator chimed, the doors opened, and out came Michael.

Kwan glared at the kid and immediately asked, "What happened?"

Michael looked shaky and scared about something. He stared at Kwan with trepidation.

"What the fuck happen, nigga?"

Michael simply handed him a note.

Kwan snatched it from the kid's hand, and Michael took off running toward the door. Something had happened. Something spooked him. Kwan immediately unfolded the note and read: *Bang! Bang! Nigga!*

Kwan's eyes opened widely. Just like he'd thought, it was a setup. But how did they know he would send the kid? More important, how did they know he was coming?

***

T-Mack, Ricky, and Holland sat there on Livonia Avenue impatiently waiting for Kwan to return. While doing so, they lit up another blunt.

Unbeknownst to them, a dangerous threat was looming their way. A dark Escalade crept in their direction with the windows down, and another threat came on foot.

Before they knew it, two black Uzis extended from the Escalade's window, and the man on foot produced a .9mm and quickly opened fire on the Tahoe, quickly overcoming T-Mack and the others with gunfire, multiple bullets tearing into their truck from both directions. There was no escape. Gunshots came from the street and the sidewalk and riddled the three men inside, jerking them violently, leaving their blood and flesh splattered onto the windows, interior, and windshield.

Quickly, the shooter on foot leaped into the Escalade, which sped off in the opposite direction.

The brutal execution in broad daylight sent people and local residents screaming and running for safety. When the smoke cleared, the Tahoe was riddled with bullets and the horror and reality of the streets was right there for everyone to see.

Kwan heard the gunfire and he quickly sped in the direction, only to see three of his men dead. He was too late. There was nothing he could do. T-Mack, Holland, and Ricky were gone. He gripped the Desert Eagle in his hand.

He looked around, thinking it wasn't over. They had to be coming for him too. But there was nothing. It was chaotic on the streets. Kwan could hear the police sirens blaring in the distance. He tucked his gun and rushed away from the crime scene. There was no telling what was coming next.

As he was fleeing the scene, he glanced to his right and noticed Cash driving a Lexus. *Was it him?* Did he have something to do with the shooting?

The sight of Cash in Brownsville looking like he was home and chilling put more of a strain on Kwan. To say that he was pissed off was an understatement. He hadn't forgotten about that nigga. It was time to put Cash back on his most-wanted list, along with Bimmy and Hassan.

# TWELVE

Kwan stormed into the New Jersey apartment fuming. It was a long, agonizing trip from Brooklyn to Elizabeth. It had all gone terribly wrong. Kwan couldn't stop thinking about the slaughter that happened a few hours earlier. He'd made it back to New Jersey by the skin of his teeth. He was sweating, paranoid, and tired. The apartment seemed empty, but hearing the shower running in the bathroom was an indication that Sophie was home.

He marched toward the bathroom, pushed open the door, and roughly pulled back the shower curtains, startling his sister. "Hurry up and get the fuck out! We need to talk!"

Sophie shouted, "Kwan, are you fuckin' crazy? I'm naked in here!"

"Just get the fuck out the shower!" he yelled before marching out of the bathroom.

Sophie knew something was wrong. The look on her brother's face was scary. She hastened her time in the shower, toweled off, made herself decent, and went into the living room to talk to him. She saw the .50-cal. on the coffee table.

Kwan was standing near the window, talking on his cell phone. "Niggas is dead!"

*Who's dead? What happened?*

"Nah, it was a setup, nigga," Kwan said.

Sophie was staying in Elizabeth, New Jersey because of the war in the boroughs. No one was safe anywhere, and Hassan had reach, with Bimmy being his outstretched hand. Elizabeth was close to the city, but a safe distance away from the war, supposedly. In Mafia terms, everyone went to the mattress.

"Kwan, what's going on?" she asked him nervously.

He ignored her question and continued talking into the phone.

"And where the fuck is that nigga Cash? I saw him there. He was around . . . Nah, fuck that! It ain't no fuckin' coincidence he was there. He was driving a Lexus."

Sophie stood and waited for Kwan to finish with his phone call.

After hanging up, he turned to her. "You talked to that nigga Cash?"

"You know he don't take my calls. And he doesn't call me back. What happened today, Kwan?"

"T-Mack, Holland, and Ricky are dead!"

"What?" Sophie was floored by the news.

"It was a setup. They got gunned down in Brownsville."

"Oh shit!"

"I got lucky. I don't know what happened, but we got set up. They knew we were coming. I wanna find that snake nigga Tony and have a serious talk wit' him, and then I'm gonna cut his fuckin' heart out and feed it to him while it still beats in my fuckin' hand. And I want you to continue reaching out to Cash."

"Was Cash really there today?"

"He was."

"You actually think he had something to do wit' today?"

"Sophie, don't be naïve! He was there, looking all smug in that fuckin' Lexus. You and I both know he was still fuckin' wit' that bitch Pearla."

Sophie looked dubious about the accusations Kwan was throwing out about the man she was once in love with. Was maybe still in love with.

The unenthusiastic look on her face caught Kwan's attention. He had an idea what was going through her head. The mention of Cash sent her into a tailspin of emotions.

"You still on that nigga's dick, ain't you?" He stepped closer to her, frustrated with his sister's emotions for a nigga who played her and used her. "Cash don't give a fuck about you!" he reminded her. "He left your fuckin' bedside that night to run and be wit' that bitch, and she already had a nigga! What you got? Shit! The nigga gotta go, Sophie, and you need to keep reaching out to that muthafucka."

"I know," she replied dryly.

He added, "We took him in, kept him alive, looked out for him, and treated him like family, and he shitted on you and me. You want a nigga like that to keep breathing?"

Sophie knew what Kwan was preaching was true. Cash had betrayed them. She loved and trusted him, and he fucked around on her with his ex-bitch. "I'll keep calling him. I'll think of something to get his attention."

"You do that."

Kwan paced around the living room, seething. He didn't know what to do with himself. Three of his best hitters were dead; it was a major setback. He had other killers on standby, but they weren't thoroughbreds like the men he'd lost today.

"What you gonna do, Kwan?" Sophie asked him.

"I'ma kill 'em all. And, Cash, I'm gonna take my time killing him."

Sophie stood there looking blank at her brother's statement. She sighed and retreated into her bedroom while Kwan busied himself with one phone call after another, preparing for battle.

Everything was starting to escalate, and she felt that it would get worse before it got better. Thinking about Cash, she wished it had worked out better between them. The sex was amazing, and she'd almost felt that their love was unconditional.

# THIRTEEN

Pearla followed the GPS instructions, crossing over the Verrazano Bridge and arriving in Staten Island. She was on her way to see Cash. Her body was tingling with anticipation. It had been two weeks since their last rendezvous. She was dressed in something simple and sexy, something sexual for the occasion—a white flirty top and white skirt, and no panties underneath. She thought about that dick and his touch. She smiled on the way he would kiss her, and the way he made her feel when things were good between them.

The traffic in Staten Island was flowing. The GPS continued to guide her south, taking Hyland Boulevard toward Eltingville. She wasn't familiar with Staten Island. It was the forgotten borough where many Mafia members resided back in the day.

She made a few turns and was two miles away from her destination. The GPS led her to a small, wooded park in the area. She parked on the quiet suburban street and killed the engine. She got out of her Benz and looked around. There was no sign of Cash.

*Why would he lead me here?* she thought.

She pulled out her cell phone and dialed his number. It rang several times before he picked up. "I'm here, Cash. Where are you?" she said.

"I'm in the park. Just follow the trail."

"Okay." She hung up and walked toward the front entrance.

As she walked into the park, a slight breeze rustled the leaves. The air was cool, and the sun was setting. The pathway she walked was strewn with rocks. Pearla tried her best to make her way in her heels. The park covered a wide area that could fit several homes, had benches everywhere, and a jogging track circled around the edge of the park.

She walked toward a bench where she saw Cash standing. She smiled at him. He didn't return her smile. She felt something was up.

"Hey, baby," she greeted him warmly. She threw her arms around him, hugging him lovingly, and could feel the butt of a gun pressing into her gut. He had a pistol tucked into his waistband.

"You alone, right?" he asked.

"Why wouldn't I be?"

"Too much shit is happening," he said.

"Like what?"

"There was a shootout yesterday in Brooklyn."

"What? Was you a part of it?"

"No. I happened to be in the area. I was just visiting my pops. But I got word that three of Kwan's men were killed."

The mention of Kwan's name sent chills running through Pearla's body. He was a scary guy. She'd heard about him and remembered when he wanted to have her kidnapped and tortured. Cash had foiled that plot, proving to her that he still loved her.

"It's too dangerous in Brooklyn, Pearla. You weren't followed, right?"

"I don't think so."

"What you mean, you don't think so? I need for you to be sure. Niggas are out there to get me, and you."

"I know, Cash."

Cash looked behind her, around her, and everywhere in the area, making sure there were no creeping goons in the bushes. There was no telling who Hassan or Bimmy hired to track them down. They could use

Pearla to get to him, if they knew the two were still seeing each other.

"I just wanted to see you, Cash. I want to be with you."

She pushed herself against him and pressed her lips against his. They kissed briefly. She was into it, but Cash seemed distracted.

"Don't worry, baby, nobody knows about us."

"You sure?"

"If they did, then I would've been a dead woman by now," she said.

Cash felt that it was all becoming too much for him—the hiding, the murders, the sneaking around and everything. Being with Pearla was starting to wrack his nerves. He knew how Hassan felt about her, and what he would do if he ever found out they were fucking again. Hassan was a cold-hearted, calculating monster. There was no telling what he knew or what he was plotting. Not only was his own life at risk, but so was his family's.

He felt foolish, thinking with his dick all the damn time. Sneaking into her home, going into enemy territory to have sex with his ex, was a suicidal act.

But that was the old Cash; the new Cash had to think rationally.

"Let's go somewhere and be together," Pearla suggested with an inviting smile, grasping his hands.

Cash sighed. He looked into her eyes. She was lovely, yes, but then he thought about the mistakes they'd made, or the ones he made. Once again, he started to feel that all of his problems were because of her. He felt that if he never went to warn her about the murderous plot against her, then Kwan wouldn't want him dead. He would still be in business with strong support. Kwan was the muscle. He was the man keeping Hassan off his ass. Now Cash had two murderous psychopaths after him, and he was hiding out like a fugitive.

"You look stressed, baby. C'mon, let me make you relax," she said. "I've been thinking about you a lot."

They walked off together, Cash keeping a vigilant eye, his gun at hand.

***

Cash looked up at the ceiling while sprawled across the motel bed, butt-naked on his back, Pearla knelt between his legs. She wrapped her full lips around his length and width, but surprisingly, he wasn't hard.

What was going on? She always made him hard. She tried to get him up with her tricks and her deep throat, but he remained limp like a noodle. She sucked and sucked, cupping his balls and then licking them, but nothing.

"Cash, what's wrong?" she asked with concern.

"I don't know. I think it's because I got a lot on my mind, Pearla."

She continued jerking his dick, hoping for some signs of life.

Though there was a first time for everything, it was embarrassing. Cash propped himself up against the headboard and stared at Pearla. She was naked too. Her pussy was wet and throbbing. The limp-dick situation wasn't working for her.

Cash sighed. "I can't do this right now," he said.

"What?" Pearla was taken aback. "Are you serious?"

"This ain't workin', Pearla."

"It ain't workin'? Two weeks ago you couldn't get enough of my pussy, and you didn't want to leave my fuckin' house. The same nigga that went down on me while Hassan was on the phone, thinkin' that shit was cute. But now I want some dick, you can't get it up. What, now you a nigga with a conscience? You have regret? Nigga, please!"

"It was stupid to do that. I don't know what I was thinkin'."

"I fuckin' came to Staten Island for nothing!" she barked.

She removed herself from the bed and put on one of his T-shirts. It angered her that she put her life on the line and put aside her pride and resentment just to be with him.

"I'm sorry."

"Fuck you, Cash! You curse me out and storm out of my place two weeks ago after I gave you some of the best sex in your life, and now you have second thoughts 'bout us?"

"I'm just worried, that's all."

"And you think you're the only one? What you think Hassan will do to me if he finds out about us?"

"What if he knows, Pearla?"

"He doesn't know about you and me, Cash," she told him. "You acted like you didn't give a fuck not too long ago. What changed?"

"I don't know. I just have been thinkin' about some things lately."

"Like what?"

Cash stood up and stood in front of Pearla with his dangling penis. Though flaccid, that muthafucka looked like gold to Pearla at the moment. She was still throbbing, and she wanted to feel him inside of her.

"You sure he don't know, Pearla? I got muthafuckas tryin' to hunt me down in every direction."

"Look, nigga, I went to see Hassan the other day, and I saw no indication that he suspected anything. In fact, the nigga had Bimmy give me ten thousand dollars. And he was still all lovey-dovey with me in that visiting room. We been careful, baby, though we had a few close calls. But I got a plan, Cash."

"A plan? Well, I got a plan too," he lied.

"You do, huh?" she replied, almost not believing him. "And what's this plan?"

"I'm still thinkin' it through."

She exhaled noisily. "Typical."

Cash had always been unstable, from the bitches he fucked with, to not knowing what he wanted. Pearla knew him like a book. Now he was worried about Hassan when he had talked so much shit before. She felt the nigga was a hypocrite. She was done talking. She was done with him.

"You know what, Cash? Fuck you again!" She stormed around the motel room collecting her things. "I have come all this way to be with you, and this is the treatment I get. Fuck you!"

She quickly got dressed. Cash sat on the bed butt-naked and showed no attempt at trying to stop her from leaving.

"What the fuck is wrong wit' you?" she hollered.

"I just need to be more cautious," he explained to her.

Out of the blue, Cash had become paranoid about Hassan and Kwan. It was just like him. Pearla wondered what spooked him. He was supposed to be gangster; now he had a change of heart about their affair.

Pearla grabbed her shit and marched toward the door, and Cash didn't even attempt to stop her. He remained in the motel room like a fool—a fucking idiot man-child.

Pearla turned around to give him one last chance to save the day. She was almost pleading to him with her eyes. Her look at him was shouting *Fix this!* But Cash was blank. He didn't want to fix it. Maybe he couldn't.

"Fuck you, Cash! I can't believe I drove out here for this bullshit!" She marched out of the room, slamming the door behind her.

Pearla walked to her car in a foul mood. She felt so stupid. Why did she keep going back to him? She needed someone to talk to.

As she climbed into her Benz, she pulled out her phone and once again tried to call April, but she wasn't answering She reasoned that April and Bimmy were still going through their issues, and that's why that bitch had been distant to her, so she decided to give her friend some space.

She felt alone. She had no one to talk to. Cash was acting weird and scared, and April was shunning her. She wiped the few tears from her eyes and drove off.

# FOURTEEN

The black-tar heroin in the balloon packaging was the absolute prize for Tony. His eyes widened at the sight of the drugs. The dealer held them out and waited for the cash transaction. Tony held out some twenty-dollar bills, totaling a hundred and forty dollars. He wanted them all. He was yearning to get high, to go into a drug binge. He wanted to buy enough drugs to last him for a week, if that. The dealer was shocked that Tony had so much cash on him. It was a first. But he didn't ask any questions. He was a drug dealer, not a detective.

Tony paid for the heroin, and the balloons were dropped into his hands. He smiled widely. The dealer pivoted and disappeared from his sight, leaving Tony looking like a kid about to walk into Disneyland. The project stairway was dim and gave Tony the privacy he needed to shoot up. The sound of a nearby door opening made him think otherwise. He decided to take the journey and walk to the shooting gallery called "Star Wars," an apartment in a nearby project building a block away. It was called Star Wars because the people in the apartment looked like they were far out of this world. Tony's only dilemma about the place was that other fiends would crowd around his treasure and want some for themselves.

Tony was a skinny black heroin addict with a tattered appearance and a knack for knowing everything that went on in the ghetto, the projects, and beyond. He was nosy and talkative. His veins were narrow and hardened from repeated heroin injections over the years. So he had to desperately and meticulously search every inch of his body for a place to plunge the syringe into. He concealed the balloons on his person and trekked down the concrete stairway and took the back exit of the project into the street.

The minute he was outside, he heard someone say, "Yo, Tony!"

Tony turned around to see who was calling him, only to be instantly struck in the face by the butt of a pistol. The blow dropped him to his knees. He cried out in pain.

Several men stood over him. Abruptly they picked him up from the ground, roughed him up, carried him to an open trunk of an idling car, and threw him inside.

"Please, don't do this!" Tony begged.

"Kwan wants to have a word wit' you," one man said.

The mention of Kwan's name made Tony's eyes become wide with fear. "Why-why he wanna see me?"

"It ain't my business. Just shut the fuck up and enjoy the ride," the man replied.

"I didn't do anything!"

"Yeah, we'll see." The man smirked down at Tony. Before the trunk was closed and he was trapped inside, his captor uttered, "We got some company for you." Out of the blue, he opened a bag with a dozen brown rats and dumped it into the trunk.

Tony screamed and squirmed as they crawled over him. He was terrified. He squealed like a bitch as the trunk was closed, leaving him in the dark with the dirty rodents and the car driving off.

Half hour later, the trunk was re-opened. The rats were having a field day with Tony, who was in tears and shaken up. But seeing Kwan glaring down at him was even more terrifying.

"Tony, Tony, Tony, the muthafucka wit' the mouth and the information," Kwan said.

"Whatever it was that you think I did, it wasn't me, Kwan. I swear to you, I didn't do it."

"Nigga, shut the fuck up!" Kwan yelled as he repeatedly punched Tony in the face, breaking his nose and spewing blood.

Kwan gestured to his man, who closed the trunk again. They could hear Tony thrashing around in the trunk, screaming and pleading to be let out. They refused to open it. Kwan wanted to torture him.

Five minutes went by, and finally the trunk was opened again. Tony was in tears and looking horror-struck.

Kwan hit him again, breaking up his face and his eye, and then he shut the trunk again. They took complete enjoyment in Tony's torment.

Ten minutes later, they opened the trunk again.

"Now listen to me, you muthafucka! Who set me up? And I swear to you, Tony, if you fuckin' lie to me or tell me some bullshit like you don't know, them rats are gonna feel like heaven once I'm fuckin' done wit' you," Kwan threatened through clenched teeth.

"Kwan, listen, please—"

"Shut the fuckin' trunk again."

"Okay! Okay! I had no choice, Kwan. You know I'm weak and I got a problem. They threatened to kill me."

"And what you think I'm gonna do to you!" Kwan shouted.

"It was Bimmy. He knew everything about me, and he told me to relay the information to you about the apartment, knowing you would go gunning for him the moment you heard the shit from me. I didn't want to do it, Kwan. But they were goin' to kill me."

Kwan was fuming. Just looking at Tony was making him angrier, and he was ready to break his neck and tear his head off from his shoulders.

"Tony, you know a lot about shit you shouldn't be knowing. So I'm gonna ask you some questions, and, nigga, don't lie to me."

"I won't, Kwan. I promise."

"Where can I find Bimmy?"

Tony was ready to utter, "I don't know." But the look on Kwan's face made him choose his words wisely. "I'm not sure where to find him, but I know where one of his peoples be at . . . a cousin of his."

"Where?"

"He fucks wit' this whore in Queensbridge."

"Tony, that's thin information. I need name and address, something to trade for your life."

"You know me, Kwan. I'm the man with the intel."

Kwan thought Tony's attempt at humor was in poor taste. "Yeah, that's what scares me about you. Keep talkin', nigga."

"I think her name is Rose, and she turns tricks out of her apartment in Queensbridge. And the cousin, they call him Run-Run. I think he was one of the shooters that day."

Kwan's blood was boiling. He was keeping his murderous behavior under control as Tony ran his mouth. He tightened his fists, stood rigid over Tony, and glared at the heroin addict.

"Yo, that's all I know, Kwan," Tony said.

"How the fuck you know so much about people's shit, Tony? Huh?"

"I just have that niche."

"That niche, huh?"

"Yeah, Kwan, but I'm down for you. Whatever you need, I'm ya nigga, fo' real."

"You a dope fiend, nigga!"

"A dope fiend wit' right intel," Tony countered.

"You know what you can do for me, Tony?" Kwan said casually.

"What's that?"

"Die, nigga!" Kwan said.

And in a heartbeat, he brandished a gun and aimed it at Tony, who became wide-eyed again, overwhelmed with fear, throwing up his hands in self-defense and pleading for his life. Kwan opened fire several times, riddling Tony's skinny body with bullet after bullet, including one that fired into his mouth, shattering several teeth.

"Stupid, talkative muthafucka—that should fuckin' shut you up for good!" Kwan slammed the car trunk on the body. "Let the rats have that muthafucka. Right now, I got a fuckin' date wit' this bitch Rose and one of her tricks."

Still clutching the smoking gun, Kwan walked away from the car and climbed into a Range Rover. It was time for some revenge in the worst kind of way.

# FIFTEEN

Hassan sat in the jail dayroom having another intense chess game with his friend Sammy. He was playing one of his best games ever. He had been on point move for move, and had Sammy on the run, his pawns down, his knights gone, and one rook standing.

But Sammy wasn't going down without a fight. He had captured Hassan's bishop and threatened with the Boden's Mate, a move in which the king, usually having castled queenside, was checkmated by two crisscrossing bishops.

Hassan was going for "Alekhine's gun," a move where the queen backs up two rooks on the same file.

Several men stood nearby quietly watching the game. The dayroom TV was on, but it was muted; both men needed to concentrate. Their authority in the jail was firm. The corrections officers didn't run anything, these two men did. The guards were simply their pawns.

Perez was watching the chess match from the sidelines. He was still awaiting his trial date. He refused to take a plea deal. He would rather take his chances in the courtroom with a well-paid lawyer.

Perez was stewing about all the failed hits and all the money he'd lost. It truly angered him that Cash and Pearla were still breathing and free to live their lives while he was rotting away. There had to be some way to kill his enemies.

When Hassan came into the jail, Perez kept his distance from him. Almost every nigga in the jail knew about Hassan. He had been putting in work for many years. Perez had a little status inside the jail too, but it was nothing compared to the notorious drug kingpin. Perez refused to ride on Hassan's dick like other inmates did, feeling the nigga was just a man. But he did feel that he and Hassan had least one enemy in common—Cash.

Perez continued to watch the chess match from a small distance, his arms folded across his chest and looking standoffish.

"Checkmate!" Hassan yelled out. He stood up proudly, and he and Sammy shook hands.

Sammy congratulated him. "Nicely done! You're definitely learning."

"I learned from the best," Hassan replied.

The mutual respect showed heavily inside the dayroom. Sammy was probably the only man Hassan looked up to and whose opinion he respected. Sammy stood up from the table and proudly left the room. He was a private man—smart and quiet all the time.

As Hassan stood among his men, another man entered the dayroom with news to tell the boss. He strolled over to the man in charge and was allowed access to Hassan. He was one of Hassan's lieutenants inside the jail, highly respected and always had his ears to the outside world.

Hassan looked his way and said, "You have some news for me, Comp?"

Comp went up to Hassan's ear and whispered, "No Kwan yet, but Bimmy and our soldiers came close. They killed three of Kwan's men the other day."

"What about Cash?"

"He's still MIA."

Hassan told him, "I don't wanna hear MIA, I wanna hear DOA."

Comp nodded.

"Get it done! I want them niggas taken care of before I come home. You understand me, Comp?"

Comp nodded.

"What about that other thing?" Hassan asked.

Knowing what Hassan was talking about, Comp replied, "It's happening right now."

"I need to have a word with Lamiek, ASAP."

"Everything's in play. His transfer to this cell block has been green-lit. He'll be here by week's end." Comp gave Hassan dap and departed from his boss.

It was the news that Hassan wanted to hear. Lamiek was his other codefendant in the case. Hassan requested his transfer closer to him, so he could politick with the nigga and have a word with him. What Hassan was asking for was best done face to face. He needed to see Lamiek's eyes, and Lamiek needed to see his.

Hassan looked reflective about a few things as he sat alone. Once again, his mind was on Pearla. He couldn't escape the feeling about her infidelity. He cringed at the thought of Cash pushing his dick into his woman while he was locked down. Thinking about it made Hassan grind his teeth and clench his fists so forcefully, he almost drew blood from his own skin.

The following day, Hassan walked into the dayroom with several of his goons. As usual, the path was cleared for him. If he wanted the TV, he had it. The weight room, it was his. The phones, the tables, the books, he had easy access to them. No one tried him. No one was stupid enough to challenge his authority.

He decided to take a seat near the TV and watch a few crime shows. He was engaging in small talk with a few of his goons, but seemed distracted.

Perez was in the dayroom. He was eager to have a word in with Hassan. He felt that he had something important that the man might want to hear. He struck up the courage to finally approach the drug kingpin and pull his coat to something. He also needed to know if Hassan had an inkling that he had anything to do with trying to murder Pearla, who at the time was Cash's girl, not his. Perez wanted to feel him out and have a simple conversation with him.

He walked toward Hassan but was quickly stopped. One man pushed his hand against Perez's chest, daring him to try and pass him.

"I just need to have a word with Hassan," Perez said casually.

"You know him, nigga?"

"Nah, just by name, but I have some news for him."

Hassan signaled his men to allow Perez to come through. He went by the protective thugs and took a seat next to Hassan. It was a tense situation for Perez. It was like he was the lone hyena and Hassan was the male lion. Both animals were vicious and carnivorous, but Hassan was the king of the jungle.

"You got three minutes, nigga. Talk!" Hassan said.

"You and me, we both from the old school, right? And Brooklyn is always gonna be our home."

Hassan didn't respond to the statement. He was just listening.

"I have nothin' but respect for you, Hassan, and I'm not tryin' to waste your time."

"Two minutes!" Hassan abruptly uttered, indicating to Perez that he *was* wasting his time with small talk.

"Look, we both have a common enemy, and that's Cash," Perez said, finally getting to the point.

Hearing Cash's name pour from Perez's mouth made Hassan lock eyes with him.

"I hate that nigga just like you. And I want him dead."

Hassan said, "Who says I want him dead?"

"C'mon, it's out there in the streets—y'all got beef! I got beef wit' the nigga too. I know he put me in here, snitching on me, that rat muthafucka!

I tried to take him out a few times, but that muthafucka got like nine lives," Perez declared in a frustrated tone.

Hassan was still listening.

"I just wanted you to know, I'm with you when it comes to killing Cash."

Hassan looked dumbfounded by Perez's words. "Yo, I don't know what you're talkin' about," he replied civilly.

Perez stared at Hassan like he was crazy. "What you mean? Cash is a problem to us both. He always gonna be a problem, Hassan. I want him dead, and I know you want him dead. I was thinkin', maybe we can help each other out."

Hassan said, "Once again, I don't fuckin' know what you're talking about. Cash is my nigga. We cool."

Hassan nodded to one of his goons, and suddenly, they all came over to Perez and instantly picked him up from his chair and patted him down like he was a snitch. For all Hassan knew, the man could be wearing a wire and trying to incriminate him for conspiracy to commit murder. It was common for inmates to snitch on other inmates to receive a reduced sentence.

Perez was clean, no wire. But Hassan was done talking to him. They kicked Perez out and warned him to stay the fuck away.

# SIXTEEN

Avery and Dalou walked out of the county jail in the early morning and thanked their blessings that they both were free men on charges of disorderly conduct. Considering their long, violent rap sheets, it was a slap on the wrist. The county jail was a familiar place to them with their many transgressions against the state of Georgia. The fight in the strip club had escalated out of control, and their actions had almost cost them ten grand. Still, they were determined to drive to New York, commit the murder, collect their pay, and have some more fun.

Avery lit a cigarette while standing outside of the courthouse. He took a few pulls and exhaled. He then looked at Dalou and said, "We need to leave town right away. I was fo' sure they were gonna keep me. A nigga got warrants." Avery knew it was human error that prevented the system from keeping him inside.

"I'm wit' ya," Dalou said.

"We need a car. That minivan ain't gonna make da trip to New York."

"What is it? Ten, eleven hours?"

"Somethin' like dat," Avery said.

"We gon' need guns too."

"I know. I'm gonna reach out to Preach, see if we can get some pistols and machine guns."

"Machine guns?" Dalou asked with a raised brow. "For one bitch?"

"Nigga, this is New York. Ain't no tellin' what we might run into in dat city."

"Fo' sure."

"You be on da car, and I'll be on the guns," Avery said.

Dalou nodded. "Let me get some of dat," he said, reaching for the Newport.

Avery took another pull and shared it with his comrade. The two were ready to leave immediately.

They walked away from the county jail cursing its existence, spitting on the ground, and tossing their middle fingers up at the place. They climbed into an idling cab nearby. It was time to earn their payday.

\*\*\*

Several hours later, Dalou pulled up to the dilapidated home in Decatur in an inconspicuous blue Ford Focus. He exited the stolen vehicle and walked into the house and saw Avery seated on an old sunken brown couch in the living room with pistols displayed on a small table.

Dressed in a wife-beater, cigarette dangling between his lips, Avery sat there inspecting each weapon. He had just come back from visiting Preach, a local gun dealer in the hood. He was able to negotiate three automatic pistols for a thousand dollars. He tried very hard to get at least one machine gun on consignment, but Preach was no fan of his. It was cash now, no credit.

"You got the car?" Avery asked Dalou.

"Yeah, it's parked outside. I picked out something nice. A Ford."

"A Ford?"

"Nigga, it was da best I could do on a last-minute thang."

Avery nodded. "Fuck it! Pack ya shit. We leavin' early tomorrow morning."

"Let's do this!" Dalou said, getting himself hyped up.

To them, it was a simple task. Drive to New York, shoot this bitch a few times, and leave. Avery promised his cousin that it was going to be a sure thing.

The two men ordered Chinese food and remained inside the entire night. They couldn't afford to get arrested again.

\*\*\*

It was two hours before dawn, and Avery was up and dressed, ready to leave Georgia. Dalou, on the other hand, was still sleeping like a baby. He was cuddled up on the mattress in the corner, snoring loudly.

Avery went over to him and kicked him awake. "Wake up, fool!" he hollered.

Dalou moved around on the mattress, hesitant to get up, but slowly opened his eyes and looked up at Avery standing over him with the .9mm tucked into his waistband.

"What time is it, nigga?" Dalou asked groggily.

"It's time fo' you to get ya ass up! We gotta hit the road. I got a bad feeling dat somethin' 'bout to come down."

"What feelin', nigga?"

"Just get ya ass up and get dressed. We got a long ride ahead of us."

Dalou lifted his drained body to his feet and moved sluggishly to get himself dressed. He had never been a morning person, and especially not when the sun wasn't even up yet. He yawned and headed for the bathroom.

Avery hurried to get their things packed into the Ford. They had everything they needed: guns, cash, and a motive to kill.

An hour before dawn, the men were pulling away from the house. Avery took the first drive. He sniffed some cocaine and was ready to soar northbound.

\*\*\*

As Avery merged onto I-20, the warrant squad came rushing to the house and kicked opened his front door. Over a dozen cops came to execute an arrest warrant for various charges, from a traffic summons to a search warrant for drugs and guns. Avery had gotten a ticket for speeding and never showed up to court. His license was suspended, and a bench warrant was issued. The search warrant for guns and drugs was executed because of a reliable snitch. The cops were very disappointed that Avery wasn't home and their search produced nothing.

The whole town knew of Avery's and Dalou's reputations, and that meant the cops did too. Anytime a horrible crime had been committed, both men were dragged into the police station for questioning. This time, the men were nowhere to be found. Lucky for them, they were on their way to New York to share some of their violent ways with the Big Apple.

＊＊＊

Several hours later, Avery pulled into a gas station a few miles outside of Greensboro, North Carolina, right off I-85. Their gas tank was running on empty. Avery had done most of the driving. The cocaine he sniffed had him up and animated. The sun was high in the sky, and the weather was warm and gentle.

Avery climbed out of the Ford smoking a cigarette, jeans sagging and his T-shirt looking soiled. His nappy hair looked even nappier. His ragged appearance was an eyesore, but he didn't care.

Dalou climbed out of the car, stretching and yawning. He had taken himself a nice nap while Avery did the driving. He looked around and saw they were in a quiet hick town. "Yo, where we at?" he asked.

"North Carolina."

"A nigga hungry as fuck," he said.

Avery turned toward him and said, "Go get me some gas. We on empty."

"How much, nigga?"

"Nigga, fill it da fuck up. It ain't like we anywhere near close to New York."

"Damn, muthafucka! Ain't you da cheery one." Dalou walked toward the gas station's convenience store.

Avery lingered near the gas pump and decided to light up another cigarette as he waited, not caring that it was dangerous to smoke at a gas station. He stared at the Waffle House across the way. His stomach was growling.

"Yo, you good, nigga!" Dalou hollered as he exited the building.

Avery started to pump the gas.

Dalou walked over and said, "Let me get some of dat," and Avery handed him the lit cigarette.

The two men stood openly as their car was being filled up.

Dalou noticed the Waffle House across the way too. "Fuckin' North Carolina. Remember the last time we were in this state, it got crazy."

"Because you were an ignorant fuck."

"Nigga, I'm ignorant? It was you who shot dat nigga in da ass because you wanted to talk to his bitch."

"Dat bitch was fine though," Avery said.

"Hells yeah! But you ain't fuck her, though."

"I ain't had the chance. Things got too crazy."

Dalou said, "You shoulda kidnapped dat bitch. I knew her pussy was probably dat good. Fuck it! We shoulda shared dat bitch."

Avery laughed.

Their gas tank was finally full. They climbed back into the Ford and went to the Waffle House. The minute they walked into the establishment, they were already being judged by the employees and customers. They took a window booth and pulled out the menus. Already they were scoping out the restaurant, and the cute waitress in the cooking area already had them drooling like hound dogs.

"Dam, dat bitch is cute," Avery said.

Dalou agreed.

She came over to take their orders, and Avery wasted no time trying to hit on her. She let it be known to them clearly that she had a boyfriend.

Avery said to her, "What ya man gotta do with me? I know you can do better."

"Excuse me?" she blurted out.

"C'mon, baby, what time ya get off? I can wait. I got one helluva a tip fo' you if you give me dat lunch special."

Avery took her hand, and she snatched it away from him. She started to get offended. It showed on her face.

Dalou instigated the situation, and before they knew it, they were making a rude scene at the Waffle House.

The manager had heard and seen enough. He marched over to their table and exclaimed, "Gentlemen, this is a restaurant, not a place to hook up. You can either order and eat your meals peacefully, or leave this place."

Avery and Dalou laughed.

"Is this nigga serious?" Dalou said.

"I will be forced to call the police," the manager said.

"Fuck you callin' da police for?" Avery shouted.

"Leave now!" the manager said in a stern voice.

Out of the blue, Avery stood up and punched him in the mouth.

The man hollered, clutching his bloody mouth, stumbling backwards.

"Someone call the police!" a customer shouted.

"We gotta go!" Dalou shouted.

The men hurried toward the exit, but a customer jumped in their way, trying to prevent them from leaving the restaurant, but Avery and Dalou weren't having it. There was no way they were going to be locked up in North Carolina.

Dalou punched him in the face, and Avery hit the man over the head with a coffee pot that was in his reach.

The man tumbled to his knees, screaming out in pain from the hot brew and shards of glass that went upside his head.

Quickly both men stomped on him, shouting, "Get da fuck outta the way, nigga!" They left him beaten.

They rushed to their car, started it up, and sped away from their violent handiwork like bats out of hell. The two men had a knack for getting themselves into brainless and ludicrous situations.

# SEVENTEEN

Cash smoked a blunt in his motel room as he watched the evening news. It was the same thing every night: murders, corruption, President Obama, and sports. Tired of the news, he turned off the television.

He focused on the blunt between his lips and relished his quiet surroundings with the .9mm by his side. He looked at the time; it was six in the evening. He was waiting for Pearla to show up. Though she'd said she never wanted to see him again, once again, her anger had subsided, and she was driving to Staten Island. Cash had promised to make it up to her.

While waiting for Pearla to come, he went to the window and briefly stared outside. The motel he was staying in was low-key and didn't have too much activity. The last thing he needed was unwanted company kicking in the front door and coming bursting into his room trying to kill everything that moved.

His eyes and ears in Brooklyn were telling him that Kwan was on a murderous rampage. He'd heard about Tony's murder. The heroin addict always had a big mouth, but this time he bit off more than he could chew by dealing with a maniac like Kwan.

There was no telling what Hassan was up to. Pearla had assured him that things were cool, but Cash couldn't escape his gut feeling that things weren't as cool as she was saying. There was too much going on out there, and he couldn't be sloppy. Cash knew it was even a risk having his Pearla come to the motel room, but he needed to keep her close because he needed information, and he needed her help. If she was as close to Hassan as she said she was, then most likely he would listen to her and respect what she had to say. But that was taking a big chance.

Cash was starting to feel lost again. Every day was the same thing, stuck in a motel room with not much to do and trying not to become too paranoid. Every car that went by he was watching. Every knock at his door made him edgy, even though it would only be the motel maid to clean his room. Everyone he came across he kept a keen eye on. And most importantly, he went nowhere without a gun, two at the least.

He finished the blunt and doused it in the ashtray on the nightstand. He continued to pace around the room. He didn't know what to do with himself. He was antsy. He thought about his father and his mother. He hated the fact that Ray-Ray was still out there begging for petty dollars and coins. He hated that his father was vulnerable to an attack from his foes, fearing that one day if they couldn't find him, then they would take their anger out on his father.

Cash had proven before that he would do anything for his pops, even kill. He hadn't seen nor heard from his mother in weeks. He had no idea where she was. Though their relationship was rocky, he still loved her.

He walked toward the window again and stared outside. He sighed. He found himself rolling up another blunt while waiting for Pearla to show up. The weed calmed him down. He needed something. Surprisingly, he wasn't having sex like that anymore, so smoking marijuana was a substitute.

He sat on the bed and inhaled. The television was still off, so the room was extra quiet. After three puffs of potent Kush, the rapid knocking at the door startled him, almost making him drop the blunt in his lap.

He jumped up and grabbed his gun and cautiously moved toward the door. He took a peek outside and saw Pearla. He sighed with relief and opened the door.

Pearla walked into the room wearing a thin jacket, tight jeans, and heels. She looked extra sexy with her long black hair flowing.

"What took you so long?" he asked.

"There was traffic."

"You came alone, right? You weren't followed?"

"Cash, you need to stop acting so shook. I'm okay. I did what you told me—sometimes do twenty miles over the speed limit, make random turns, and constantly look into my rearview mirror. Believe me, I'm alone. No one is following me."

Pearla started to feel that she'd liked him better when he wasn't paranoid, when he was bold and arrogant, and a fuckin' sex maniac. This new Cash, the one always on guard and alert, was starting to irritate her. But she'd come a long way from her home.

Cash shut the door. He still had the gun in his hand.

Pearla looked down at it and said, "Baby, you're not going to need that thing. Put it away."

Cash nodded. He placed the gun on the nightstand. "You went to see Hassan again?" he asked.

"Not this week."

"What about Bimmy? He's been by your place recently?"

"No, he hasn't."

Pearla unzipped her jacket and removed it from around her and tossed it onto the bed. The top she wore was tight and flattering.

Cash's eyes lingered on her clothes. She always had good taste in clothing. She knew how to stand out. It was one of the things he loved about her.

Pearla walked closer to him. She wanted to hug him. She wanted to feel him, and kiss him. She wanted so much from him, the nasty and the good. She looked in his eyes. "Why can't I fuckin' quit you, Cash?"

"I don't know," he simply replied.

"You do shit to me that I hate. But every time, I forgive you and come back to you like it's a new day."

They looked at each other seriously. He took her hands into his. When they'd first met, and had sex, it was fireworks twenty-four-seven. It felt like they would always love each other and have each other's back. Well, that was what Pearla had predicted. But their relationship had been so rocky, it felt like a few more hard bumps and they would be knocked off the road.

"What you think we should do?" Cash asked.

"What?"

"What was your plan? The last time you were here, you said you had a plan."

"Well, what about your plan? You said you had a plan too. Why does it always have to be me who saves the day?"

"What day you saving?" Cash asked, insulted. "I had a plan, but it fell through."

Pearla didn't want to talk about a plan, not now anyway. Maybe after sex. But why did he want to know about her plan? It bothered her. Did he only want to see her because he was looking for an escape route from the danger surrounding him?

*If push comes to shove, would he take a bullet for me? Would he? Would he sacrifice his well-being for mine?* "I don't want to talk about no plan right now, Cash."

"I just wanted to talk to you."

"You coulda done that over the phone. I came here to be with you."

"I know."

"Don't do this to me, Cash. I can't continue to become your fuckin' puppet. You just can't always have things your way. What the fuck I look like to you—Burger King?"

"Nah, you don't."

"Whatever moves you're gonna make, Cash, you need to do them on your own. I've always tried helping you."

"I know."

"I believed in you. I loved you," she said from the heart. "Did you ever love me just the same? Or was I just an opportunity for you? Huh, Cash?"

"No woman could ever compare to you, Pearla, but you know me, I'm a fuckup. Sometimes I wonder how you could ever love a nigga like me."

She looked at him, trying her best to hold back the contempt from engulfing her. Love was hurtful, but Cash was a fuckin' train wreck. He had always been dangerous, starting with her heart and her emotions.

Unexpectedly, Cash asked, "You ever wondered who tried to have us killed that day at the house?"

"Of course, I did, Cash. But I try not to dwell on it."

"Why not? Whoever hired them shooters, they're still out there."

"I can't live my entire life in absolute fear, Cash. Yes, I'm cautious, and I watch over my shoulders, but I'm not like you. I can't just live out some motel room in the boondocks. I want to enjoy things—enjoy success and love. I want to be rich and free, and I'm going to keep moving forward, no matter what it takes."

"And you think I don't want the same thing?"

"Cash, most times I don't fuckin' know what you want."

"I don't wanna die, that's for sure."

"And I don't want you to die."

"So I need for you to do me a favor," he said.

*A favor?* she thought. Did he have the audacity to ask her for a favor, after everything he was putting her through?

"You know my beef wit' Kwan is because of you. I went against him only to protect you, Pearla."

"And I am grateful, Cash, and have shown you in so many ways. I'm risking my life just by being here, ready to please you."

"I know."

"Do you?"

"Listen, I'm asking you to have a word with Hassan and let him know that I'm tired."

"Tired?" she asked with a raised eyebrow. "Tired of what?"

"I just want to end my beef wit' him. Squash it all."

"And how am I supposed to do this?"

"Let him know that his beef isn't wit' me, but wit' Kwan. And that I saved your life from him."

Pearla remembered the last time she took up for Cash. Hassan had slapped her so hard, she could still feel the grueling tingle from his hand against her face. No, she wasn't getting involved.

"I can't do that, Cash."

"Why not?" he replied, looking angry at her response.

"I won't do it. We make our own choices and paths, and you've made yours, and I'm making mines with Hassan. And you know what? He's been there for me when you weren't."

"Well, you need to explain to him that you and I, we're nothing more than friends. And you were supposed to be my friend and have my back, Pearla."

Hearing Cash refer to her as nothing but a friend hurt her, cut her deeply in the heart. It only brought up bad memories of when he'd left her alone in their Jamaica Estates home, knowing there were people out there trying to kill them.

Pearla gave Cash a long look of disappointment and shook her head. Finally, the blindfold was off, and she saw him for who he truly was—a self-centered asshole and grimy prick who'd dug his own hole.

"I'm done," she announced to him loud and clear.

"Done?"

"You don't want me, and you don't love me. You never did. I'm just mad at myself for not seeing it sooner."

Cash frowned. He didn't like what he was hearing.

Pearla picked up her things and said, "You get yourself out of your own troubles. I'm gone!"

She marched out of the motel room and didn't look back, leaving Cash standing there looking dumbfounded. She got into her Benz and vowed to never come back. He was no longer worth the effort.

# EIGHTEEN

Hassan sat in his small jail cell reading *The Art of War* by Sun Tzu. He was fully into the book, trying to become distracted from his confined environment. He read about how Sun Tzu emphasized the importance of positioning in military strategy. Hassan thought about his own army and his war with Kwan. Hassan felt there was little he could do while incarcerated on Rikers Island. The book was helpful and it was entertaining. With his face in the book and his attention on the chapter describing detail assessment and planning, a corrections officer called out for his attention.

"Hassan, he's here."

Hassan looked up to see the stout African American guard escorting Lamiek to his cell.

"You have ten minutes with him," the guard said. "Then I gotta take him back to his area."

"I'll only need five minutes, Jason," Hassan replied.

"Cool." The corrections officer nodded then turned and walked away, leaving Lamiek behind for Hassan to have a word with.

Lamiek stood at the border of the cell, looking intimidated and tense. Hassan fixed his eyes on his codefendant. His look alone was chilling.

Lamiek was a frail character with a bald head and hard eyes. His body was enveloped with tattoos, his arms thin like strings. But what he lacked in physicality, he made up for in sheer heart. Though he was a menace and a warrior on the streets, to Hassan, he was a simple subordinate.

"Yo, come in, nigga. I need to talk to you," Hassan said.

Lamiek slowly walked closer to Hassan. "What's good, Hassan?"

"Have a seat."

Lamiek chose to stand rather than take a seat on the same cot as Hassan. He remained cool, though he had an inkling why Hassan wanted to see him.

"I know you heard about Wayne-Oh," Hassan said.

"Yeah, I did. I'm sorry he went out that way. He was a good dude."

"He was."

"So why I'm here?"

"Lamiek, you always have been a ruthless nigga in Brooklyn. Your name does ring out."

"Not like yours, boss."

"It doesn't, do it?" Hassan replied, almost mocking his soldier.

Hassan stood up. He outweighed the young boy by sixty pounds. He locked his eyes into the man's. Lamiek was his last choice.

Lamiek knew that Hassan would be a fool to kill him, ensuring he would most certainly take the weight for the guns and the bodies if he was the last one standing. But he also knew that Hassan was diabolical and, if pushed, would certainly have him murdered then face the consequences with a good lawyer.

"You know why I've called you to my cell, right?"

"I have an idea."

"You see, we, or shall I say I, have this dilemma, and you are my solution."

Lamiek frowned. He was a young dude, just barely twenty years old. No one wanted to go to jail for life. Period! But he didn't want to die either.

"I have two kids, Hassan," he informed his boss.

"You do, huh?"

"Yeah, they're two and three, and I want to see them grow up."

"That's nice," he replied dryly. "You're a good father, I see."

"I try to be."

"I respect that. But I need you to respect this, too," Hassan said casually. "I'm a businessman, you understand me?"

Lamiek nodded. "I do."

"And you're a killer, nigga, and that's what we needed in my organization. Your lethal ass, if lucky, would have had a few more years left on the streets before you would have gotten murdered. You were too reckless, Lamiek, with your hothead ass, and it was only a matter of time before your two kids would see their father no more."

Lamiek knew Hassan was telling the truth. He had a fierce and deadly temper. He was a hothead. He had a lot of bodies under his belt, and he was constantly dodging the law, with numerous warrants for his arrest, always on the run or hiding out because whenever a murder happened everyone suspected it was Lamiek. Also, he couldn't stay out of those seedy after-hour spots, and he was always "blunted," making it too easy to catch him slipping.

Hassan continued to talk while Lamiek just stood there and listened.

"On the streets, you benefited my organization profoundly with your gun. Now in here, I'm gonna need you to help benefit my organization in a different manner, by showing me loyalty."

"Loyalty," Lamiek repeated.

"Yes, loyalty, Lamiek. Besides, how can a dead man raise his kids?"

Lamiek just stood stoically.

"I have a proposition for you, Lamiek . . . a very favorable one toward you and your two kids."

"I'm listening," Lamiek said quietly.

"Good. You always have been a smart man, and you know where this is leading. I'm gonna need you to cop out to the charges—plead guilty to the guns and the murders. You let the prosecutors know that I had nothing to do with anything. I'm an innocent man. In exchange for this, I'll help you. I'll take care of you and your family, whoever—your kids, your mother, your baby mammas—one million dollars to you or them.

"Of course, it wouldn't be all at once. It will be in installments. You will receive two hundred thousand when my charges are dropped and I'm released at my next bail hearing. Then there will be another four hundred thousand when you're sentenced to these charges. Afterwards, forty thousand a year to your family for the next several years for your loyalty to this organization. We won't forget you, Lamiek." Hassan hooked his cold eyes onto Lamiek, waiting for his reply.

Reluctantly, he agreed. "Okay."

Hassan smiled. "Like I said, you've always been a smart man and always showed loyalty to this organization."

Lamiek was smart enough to keep his comments to himself. He had sold his soul to the devil a long time ago. What was he to do or supposed to say? Money or no money, the answer had to be yes. He didn't want to become Wayne-Oh, part two. And then Bimmy was a major threat to his family in the streets. He thought about his kids and his family, and the sacrifice had to be made.

"We done here?" the guard asked.

"Yes, we're done here," Hassan said.

Lamiek turned around and left the cell with the guard. The only positive thing he could think about was that his family would be taken care of financially. He only hoped Hassan would keep his word and pay out the money, once he ate the murder and gun charges and gave his life away to the state.

\*

Several hours later, with the lights out and the majority of the inmates in Rikers Island sleeping, Lamiek was wide awake, staring at the bland jail walls. The hardcore gangster and killer found himself crying in the dark.

# NINETEEN

That's that nigga right there, Kwan," Asher pointed out, watching a young black male with long dreadlocks climb out of a black Audi A4 on 41st Avenue in Queensbridge.

Kwan nodded and took a drag from the cigarette in his mouth. He kept a clear eye on Bimmy's cousin, the nigga named Run-Run, one of the higher-ups in Hassan's organization. They were parked right across the street from the building he was going into. So far, Tony's information was on point. But Kwan was still skeptical. He remembered the last time he and his men were about to make a move, and it blew up in his face. This time, he came to Queensbridge with two carloads of men armed to the teeth and ready for anything coming their way. Kwan's head continuously swiveled back and forth, not wanting to be the victim of another ambush.

Queensbridge Houses was the largest public housing project in the United States. Kwan was there to execute someone—but not before he and his men got him to talk—to make a very violent statement.

Run-Run went into the six-story building to see his bitch for the day. He didn't know he was being watched. The man was dressed immaculately, sporting a leather jacket, bright Timberland boots, and gold jewelry. He had a clean-shaven face and beautiful dark skin. Run-Run looked more like a GQ model than a thug.

When he walked into the lobby, Kwan and several of his comrades stepped out of their vehicles, their guns concealed.

Kwan said, "Yo, y'all three come wit' me, and the rest of y'all keep an eye out for anything. If it moves wrong, then fuck 'em up. I'm not tryin' to make the same mistake again."

Kwan, Asher, and the other goons crossed the street and went into the building lobby. They already knew which floor and which apartment Rose stayed in. The unfamiliar faces to the local residents in the neighborhood stormed into the stairway and hurried toward the third floor. They were itching to start chaos and pandemonium inside the project apartment. It was time for some serious payback.

Kwan's crew picked the lock and stealthily entered the apartment.

***

"Oh shit! Oh shit! Damn, you feel so good," Run-Run proclaimed as he thrust his dick into his number-one bitch from the back.

Rose leaned over the long dresser, grabbing it securely with her legs spread and her phat ass wiggling in the air.

Run-Run grabbed her thick hips and continued pounding her. The deep penetration felt so good to them both. He played with her tits and smacked her ass. Rose liked it rough, and they both liked it doggy-style while standing up.

"Fuck me! Yes! Fuck me!" Rose screamed out.

Kwan could hear the sexual activity coming from the bedroom. Kwan, T-Mack, Holland and Ricky all had their guns out. Gradually, the men moved toward the bedroom. The door was ajar. He peeked inside and could see Run-Run fucking the whore doggy-style, both their backs toward the door.

Kwan and his goons burst into the bedroom and completely took Run-Run and Rose by surprise. Run-Run jumped out of the pussy and tried to reach for his gun on the nightstand, but he was too late. A crowd of goons jumped on him, quickly pistol-whipping him and beating him to the ground.

Rose screamed, but Kwan immediately ended her vocals with a swift punch to the face, followed by a harsh, "Shut the fuck up, bitch!" and she tumbled off the bed and hit the floor. To Kwan, it was a sweet thing to see—people's pain.

Run-Run was butt-naked on the floor. He scowled up at his attackers. "Y'all niggas are dead!"

Kwan shouted, "What, bitch? You got the nerve to threaten us?"

Kwan glared down at Run-Run and couldn't help himself. The sight of Bimmy's cousin infuriated him. He gripped his pistol tightly and went to work on the side of Run-Run's head with the butt of the gun. The side of Run-Run's head started to look like the color of crimson, and his eye had been split open with a deep gash. Kwan tried to control himself, but thinking about that day made him mad.

Asher had to pull Kwan off Run-Run before he killed him too soon. "We still need him to talk, Kwan."

Kwan was breathing heavily. The urge to blow his head off was so strong, Kwan almost had an erection in his pants. Asher was right, though; they'd come there for information first, and then they could kill the nigga right after. "Yo, take that nigga into the fuckin' bathroom," he said.

They picked Run-Run up from the floor. He tried to resist, but he was beaten again, and they dragged him into the small bathroom to handle their business.

Kwan looked down at the naked whore on the floor. She was cowering in the fetal position, scared to death.

"Yo, Kwan, let me get some of that," one of his goons said, thirsty to bust a nut.

"Nigga, we ain't here for that. Watch that sneaky bitch. She move, kill her." Kwan then marched toward the bathroom with some devious shit planned for Run-Run.

The volume to the stereo inside the apartment was turned all the way up, blaring today's rap songs.

Run-Run's blood coated the white tiled floor. He was on his knees and defeated. Kwan's hands were layered with his blood, as he opened up Run-Run's flesh with a serrated knife. Then there were cigarette burns to his skin, and a few of his fingers were broken. Still, the nigga wasn't talking. He was a tough muthafucka, refusing to give up any information on his cousin.

While Run-Run was being tortured, his whore was being mentally tortured. Niggas were in her ear telling her that she was about to die slowly for fucking the wrong nigga, asking her to beg for her life.

"This nigga ain't talkin', Kwan. Fuck it."

Kwan still wanted some information on Bimmy. Anything. But the cousin was showing true loyalty. If Kwan didn't hate the nigga, then he would've respected his "gangster." But he was never one to just give up so easily; something had to break this nigga.

Another half-hour later, they found Run-Run's breaking point—his kids. In his wallet there was his license with his address. Kwan threatened that if he didn't talk, then he would go to his place and murder his entire family, starting with the baby mama, and then the kids.

"Nigga, I swear, I'm gonna eat ya fuckin' kids and shit them out if you don't tell me somethin' about Bimmy."

That broke Run-Run, and he talked.

It was the end of him. Kwan cut his throat from ear to ear, and he bled out like a pig. His body lay mutilated and naked on the bathroom floor.

Then it was the whore's turn to die. Kwan took Rose into a chokehold and squeezed the life out of her. He broke her neck too, and she dropped dead.

# TWENTY

Bimmy sat across from Hassan in the visiting room frowning and upset about the loss of his little cousin, Run-Run. He and Run-Run grew up together on the mean streets of Brooklyn, New York, and were like brothers. Bimmy had taken his little cousin under his wing years earlier and groomed him for the game. The love was real. Run-Run was family, not like Avery, who was a perpetual fuckup. Though Avery was Bimmy's cousin too, he wasn't family.

The news hit Bimmy like a ton of bricks. It hurt him. It was unbelievable, but it was real. How did they get to him? How did they know about the whore? Bimmy had underestimated his rival. It was now time to go into overdrive.

"They didn't have to do him like that," Bimmy said. "They did him bad."

"We gonna find that muthafucka, Bimmy," Hassan said quietly, "and we gonna slaughter him."

Bimmy was in a foul mood. He ached even more to find Kwan, or anyone associated to him, and kill them slowly.

"You know I loved him like a brother, Bimmy. He was a good man."

"Cash, we find him first. I want him!"

"You've been lookin' for the nigga for a while, and he ain't come out of his hole yet."

"What about Pearla?" Bimmy asked.

"What about her?"

"She can find that nigga for us. She can pull that muthafucka out of his hole. She does it all the time."

"What? No!"

"Why not, Hassan? This nigga Kwan gotta go now."

"You don't bring Pearla into this. She has no connection to Cash," Hassan said.

"And you're absolutely sure about that?"

"Nigga, I'm sure!"

Bimmy frowned even harder. Hassan was an ass. Of course, Pearla had a connection to Cash—She was fucking the nigga. His boss couldn't see it. Bimmy wanted to follow Pearla. Maybe that bitch would lead him to Cash.

Once he found Cash, he would find Kwan, though word on the streets was Cash and Kwan were beefing with each other. Anyhow, Cash was still a valuable nigga. Bimmy was going to make him talk, find out the people close to Kwan, and then murder both those muthafuckas.

Hassan said, "I'll pay for Run-Run's funeral, no expenses spared. You send him off real good, Bimmy. Your cousin was definitely loved and respected."

Bimmy was grateful, but paying for the funeral didn't appease his hunger for revenge. He was burning up inside. There was nowhere Kwan or Cash could hide. He was determined to find them.

"But I got good news," Hassan said, changing the subject. "My lawyer was able to get me another bail hearing . . . next week."

"That's good news," Bimmy said dispassionately.

"It is. I told you that these muthafuckas ain't gonna keep me in here. I'll be home soon. My lawyer is working everything out on his end, and I took care of everything on my end."

Bimmy nodded, ambivalent about Hassan's release. It could be trouble for him if Avery fucked up, or Hassan getting out could be beneficial. Who knew?

The hour visit went by, and Bimmy felt slighted by Hassan's lack of sympathy for Run-Run. If it had been Pearla or anyone in his family, Hassan would be beside himself. There would be no stopping his wrath. But Hassan was more concerned with his upcoming bail hearing and Pearla than with trying to annihilate the foes plotting against them. Hassan had changed since he'd been locked up. Bimmy knew it, felt it, and needed to do something about it.

He walked out of the jail and got on the bus that took visitors to the parking lot, frowning the entire time. He was aching to kill someone.

The minute he stepped off the bus and walked toward his car, he pulled out his cell phone and made a call.

The phone rang several times before Avery answered, "Yeah, cuz?"

"Where the fuck you at?"

"We still on 95, 'bout five hours away."

"You should have been here days ago!"

"I know. Had a few mishaps though, but it's all taken care of. We on our way."

"The moment you get to New York, you call me. You understand?"

"Got ya."

"I want that bitch dead by the week's end," Bimmy growled.

"She will be, cuz. I assure you dat."

Bimmy hung up. Now he definitely had a motive to kill Pearla. He was willing to do what Hassan was too weak to do. Bimmy thought when Cash received the news about Pearla's murder, it would bring him out of hiding. That's when Bimmy's goons would snatch him up and have a serious and rough talk with the nigga. Then they would find pieces of him all over New York, one week at a time.

***

Avery and Dalou stopped to get some gas in Randallstown, Maryland, a predominantly African American suburb in Baltimore County, about twenty miles away from Baltimore. Not only were they low on gas, but, worse, they were out of weed. They were getting bored and restless.

Dalou took his turn driving. He was itching to smoke a blunt. It was late afternoon, and they were about four hours from New York. They felt that they had some time to kill. It was time to explore Baltimore County and find some weed to purchase.

Dalou drove down Liberty Road and pulled into a gas station. Both men climbed out of the Ford Focus and looked around. It was quite a busy area: numerous gas stations, stores, and neighborhood businesses around. Traffic was moving.

Avery lit a cigarette. They needed something to get their bodies going, if not weed, then some pills or cocaine. "Put twenty-five down on pump seven," he told Dalou.

He nodded.

Dalou walked toward the building.

Avery lingered by the pump, observing every car coming and going and locking his eyes on every male or female. He was looking for who had that look to approach and maybe ask the right thing to get them the right score.

He fixed his eyes on the old Chevrolet pickup truck that drove into the gas station and stopped at the pump across from him. The driver got out, a young white boy. He was thin, dressed raggedly in stained denim jeans, worn work boots, and a flimsy black T-shirt that said, *Alcohol, Tobacco, Firearms—Who's bringing the chips?* He wore a plaid hunter's cap and sported a scraggly beard. Everything about him screamed "drugs" to Avery. If not weed, then maybe crystal meth.

Avery watched him go into the gas station and come right back out.

He reached for the gas pump and started to put gasoline into his old pickup. Avery knew it was now or never. Dalou was still in the store doing God knew what.

"Funny shirt. I really like it," Avery said, chuckling.

The young redneck glanced at Avery and said, "Thanks."

"I'll bring da chips, I'm just short of da tobacco, if ya know what I'm sayin' to you, friend."

The young boy looked at Avery. He was unsure about him. "Where you from?" the boy asked.

"De Dirty South. Georgia."

"I can hear your accent."

"It's that noticeable, huh?"

"It is."

"I have a crisis," Avery started. "Me and my friend had a long trip, and we on our way north, but we just need one thang. We need a little pick-me-up, ya know. We need to get on dat white horse, or tweek maybe, and ya look like a guy dat can help us out."

"Huh?"

Avery knew something that would get his attention. He pulled out the cash. It was the only clue he needed.

"Oh, *that* pick-me-up," the redneck said.

"I'm willing to pay for it. You know somebody?"

He smiled. "I do."

"Then problem solved," Avery said, smiling too. "I'm Avery."

"Adam."

Dalou walked out of the store with a bag filled of junk food and things. He was caught off-guard by Avery talking to the white boy in the funny T-shirt.

"Dalou, this is Adam, and he's our new best friend," Avery said.

Dalou quickly caught on.

The duo followed behind Adam in his pickup with Avery driving. The duration of the ride they were plotting something sinister. They drove deeper into the country area, away from the county.

Dalou looked at Avery and said, "So, we gonna rob dis redneck white boy, right?"

"If he got da right shit. Yeah!"

"What he got?"

"Don't know yet. We'll see when we get thurr."

Both men were anxious. They needed something potent in their systems. They wanted to get high like yesterday. But there was no way they were going to pay for it, especially to some white-trash, redneck white boy in a beat-up truck. To them, he was easy prey. He seemed stupid. He was the perfect mark. The farther they drove away from a heavy populated area, the better it was for them.

Forty minutes after meeting Adam at the gas station, the men were in a place called Finksburg, Maryland. Adam led them to a small, shotgun-looking home somewhere in the backwoods of Maryland. The old house looked like it was about to collapse inwardly on itself. The roof sagged, and the cedar shingles stuck up in places like wonky teeth. There was nothing but trees, high bushes, and dirt roads all around. The front yard of the run-down home was cluttered with old junk cars and outdated machinery that looked over fifty years old. The grass was uncut and unkempt. It was a redneck's paradise.

Adam climbed out of his pickup, and Avery and Dalou climbed out of their Ford. They looked around.

Dalou joked, "We ain't in Kansas anymore, huh?"

Avery didn't find him humorous. He just wanted to get what they came for and leave.

"Y'all gon' want to meet with my brother, Henry. He has just what y'all boys are lookin' for," Adam said.

"Boys?" Dalou repeated, somewhat offended by the word.

"Just chill. We in and we out."

All three men walked into the house. Inside was even worse than the outside. The furniture was old-fashioned and dusty. The wood floors were creaky and unstable. Inside reeked of cigarettes and garbage. The paint on the walls was chipped, and the windows were falling apart. It was worse than their place in Georgia.

The screen door shut behind Dalou. Adam shouted, "Henry, we have us some company."

The men stood in the living room. They both were armed with pistols and waiting for the right time to make their move. So far, it looked simple—two white boys that wouldn't even see it coming.

Henry loomed from the kitchen in the back. He was a big boy with swollen arms, dressed in a soiled wife-beater with a hairy torso and a scraggly beard that matched his brother's.

Henry was tall and looked to weigh close to three hundred pounds. He stared at the two black males in his home and asked his brother, "Adam, who these boys?"

Once again, Dalou felt offended by the use of "boys." He kept silent, though.

"They're looking for drugs," Adam said.

"Drugs?" Henry said, arching his eyebrows.

"They came a long way to score some meth," Adam said.

Henry looked at them and asked, "Y'all boys smoke meth? Y'all two look more like weedheads to me."

"We just hurr to score something to get us by and leave," Avery said.

Slyly, Avery did a once-over of the place. It appeared that Adam and Henry were the only occupants of the house.

"Something to get you boys by, huh?"

"Yeah, something to get us by. We still got a long drive ahead."

"And do you boys have the cash?"

"First, what ya sellin'?"

"Crystal meth and cocaine."

"Cocaine," Avery repeated, shocked that he had some blow. "Coke is A-Okay for us."

"How much cash?" Henry asked.

Avery pulled out his small wad of bills, which had been dwindling since they'd started their trip. He had about nine hundred dollars on him.

Henry smiled heavily. He had a toothless smile. He stared at Avery, and the two locked eyes with each other. Avery automatically knew that the redneck wasn't as dimwitted as his younger brother.

"That is a lot of cash. How much you need?"

"Whatever ya got, we'll take it," Avery said.

Henry looked at Adam and then said, "Adam, go and get these boys the royal treatment. Them some paying folks."

Adam nodded and disappeared from the room, while Henry stood around to keep them company.

Avery and Dalou glanced at each other. They read each other, knowing what to do once the drugs came into their view. It was going to be show time.

"So, y'all boys are from Georgia, hey?" Henry said, trying to make small talk while they waited for the goods.

"Yeah, we from da South."

"It can get really hot down there. I know. My family is from Alabama."

"That's good to know."

Avery was becoming impatient. Adam was taking too long. "Where's ya brother? What's takin' him so long?" he asked.

"You know, that's a good question. Let me go and find out. You boys stay put now, okay?" Henry walked away, leaving the two men alone.

"Yo, somethin' don't feel right, Avery," Dalou said.

Avery agreed. Things felt too still for him.

They looked around the shabby home and suspected their plan to rob these rednecks was coming unhinged.

"We should leave," Dalou suggested.

"They got somethin' in this fuckin' shithole." Avery wanted to leave, but at the same time, he wanted to score some drugs. He was itching to get high. He didn't want to have to come so far out of the way for nothing. *Keep your eyes on the prize*, he told himself.

*Chk-chk.*

The dreadful sound of a shotgun being pumped sent the men into a panic. That sound was never good. It came from a neighboring room.

Avery and Dalou knew it was time to react and go on the defense. They quickly pulled out their pistols just in time.

Adam came charging out a room with a double-barrel shotgun. He was gunning for them shouting, "You niggers better give us that cash! You think we some stupid rednecks!"

"Fuck you!" Avery shouted. He fired—*Bam! Bam! Bam!*

Just like that, chaos ensued.

Adam shot off a round that barely missed both men and created a large hole in the wall behind them.

They hid behind the old, dusty furniture in the room that provided little cover. But it was better than nothing.

Henry came charging into the room with his shotgun too. He took aim at the men and fired. The blast was loud, and it shattered a few pieces of furniture near the men.

"We just want the money, you niggers. Y'all can leave with y'all lives!" Henry shouted.

"*Niggas!*" Dalou shouted.

"Fuck you, you fat cracker-ass redneck muthafucka!" Avery shouted. "You come a step closer, and I'm gonna shoot da gravy out ya ass!"

"Okay, you niggers had y'all chance!" Henry shouted.

He aimed and fired. It was his second miss. They were pinned down in the corner, but not for too long. Avery looked at his partner in crime. They were both ready to go hard or go home. There was no way they were going to die tonight—not by the hands of some ignorant, shotgun wielding rednecks.

Adam charged forward, eager to receive his payday. Nine hundred dollars was a lot of money, and he was ready to take it from a dead nigger's body.

Adam took a step closer, leaving himself open to attack. Avery sprung to his feet, aimed, and lit him up. *Bam! Bam! Bam! Bam!*

Each shot was a direct hit. The hot slugs tore into Adam center mass and pushed him off his feet. He was dead before he hit the ground.

Henry screamed frantically. He had just witnessed his little brother killed right in front of him. "You fuckin' niggers! I'm gonna kill you niggers!" he shouted.

"Bring it, muthafucka!" Dalou yelled.

Henry charged at the men, firing wildly at them.

Avery and Dalou were still alive, and Henry was out of ammo. The two men stood up from their protective place and smirked at him. He was helpless now.

"Yeah, nigga, you done fucked up now," Dalou mocked.

They aimed at the fat, country, racist redneck and lit him up like a Christmas tree. He dropped like heavy timber falling in the forest.

Both men wiped the sweat from their brows and thanked their lucky stars. Shit got intense so fast, but they were alive.

"Check their pockets," Avery said. "I know they got somethin' on dem."

Though they were in the backwoods, there was no telling who heard the gunfire and called the police. Dalou quickly rummaged through the men's pockets, and bingo, they found a small amount of crystal meth and weed on Henry. It wasn't much, but it was something for them. They fled the crime scene, jumped into the Ford, and Avery drove away.

However, they had one problem. The sun was setting, and they had no idea where they were.

As if things couldn't get any worse, Avery's cell phone rang, and it was Bimmy. Avery knew Bimmy was upset.

# TWENTY-ONE

t took long enough, but Avery and Dalou were finally in New York. They crossed over the Verrazano Bridge into Brooklyn and took the Brooklyn-Queens Expressway deeper into Brooklyn. From Georgia to the Big Apple was one hell of a trip.

It was twilight, and traffic in the city was thick because of construction and an accident on the highway. Dalou was driving, while Avery sat back in the passenger seat and pulled on a blunt. The city was full of life. Every square inch of the city was vibrant with activity. Avery couldn't remember the last time he'd been there.

The moment they touched down in Brooklyn, he took out his cell phone and called Bimmy to let him know they'd finally arrived.

The phone rang several times until Bimmy picked up. He sounded impatient with his cousin, saying, "Y'all niggas in New York yet?"

"Yeah, we hurr, cuz. What ya need us to do?" Avery asked.

"Nigga, check into a fuckin' motel and get y'all selves straight. And then call me when y'all get settled."

"Okay, cuz."

Bimmy hung up. He liked his conversations nice and short. He was never a phone person. Now that his cousin was in town, it was time to expedite his plan, especially now that Hassan was having a bail hearing soon and there was a strong chance that he might be coming home.

Dalou drove toward the Canarsie section of the borough, following the GPS instructions, on their way to a Motel 6. They moved through Brooklyn easily and arrived at the motel just before midnight. They checked in with no problems. The room was nice and comfortable, and the area of Brooklyn that they were in was tranquil and far away from any trouble in the ghetto. The last thing they needed was trouble when they were so close to a ten-thousand-dollar payday.

Avery nodded in approval. "Yeah, I can definitely get used to this," he said. They had cable TV, clean bathrooms, and twin beds. What they needed next was some weed and some bitches.

Dalou took a seat on one of the twin beds and soon spread out. It had been a long and exhausting trip, during which they'd murdered two people and assaulted a man and manager at the Waffle House.

While Dalou went to sleep, Avery lit another cigarette and stared out the window. He felt good to be in New York to put in some work for his cousin. This was the big leagues, and he was determined not to fuck it up. He wanted to show his older cousin he was capable of becoming a hit man for the organization. He wasn't going to think twice about that bitch they were going to kill. Whoever she was, she was a dead bitch! She was his chance to propel himself toward becoming somebody. Who knew? If the hit went as planned, New York could become their permanent home.

***

It was the middle of the night and the hard knocking at the door woke up Avery and Dalou. Both men jumped out of bed, looking somewhat startled. It sounded like police, but they doubted it.

Avery grabbed his gun and went to the door cautiously. He looked through the peephole and relaxed when he saw Bimmy. He opened the door.

Bimmy walked inside forcefully. "Why y'all niggas so late?" he barked.

"Car trouble," Avery lied.

Bimmy stared at his cousin and then Dalou, two country niggas looking for a breakthrough in the criminal life. Everything about them was completely off in Bimmy's eyes, from their clothes to their accents. They were an embarrassment to him. Avery looked like a nightmare. Bimmy had seen bums that looked less sloppy. His ashy cousin looked like he didn't know how to wash his own ass. If his was the last face someone saw before they died, God help them.

Bimmy hoped that his city didn't eat them alive before they did what they needed to do. He hadn't seen his cousin in years. He didn't miss him, and it wasn't a family reunion. Avery was just part of his master plan.

"Y'all ready for this? Because I can't have any fuckups. Y'all niggas understand me?"

"Believe me, cuz, we were born ready," Avery replied.

Bimmy saw the guns in their hands and the looks in their eyes. They both looked thirsty and ready, but also like two fools standing in their underwear. He knew his cousin was a no-good troublemaker back in Decatur. His name rang out there. But this wasn't the country. This was New York, always moving and nothing to play with. One wrong move, and it could be their last.

But Bimmy needed out-of-town shooters. He couldn't take any chances with Pearla's murder being linked back to him. Hassan had never met Avery, and Bimmy had never talked about any of his family in the South.

Bimmy handed them a clear and glossy eight-by-ten picture of Pearla.

"Damn! She's pretty," Avery commented.

Dalou admired the picture too. They looked like two horny hound dogs drooling over Pearla's pretty photo.

Bimmy shook his head. "I want y'all to kill her, not fuck her."

Avery nodded.

Bimmy handed them a list of all the known locations she frequented. First, a hair salon in the city that was supposed to be safe. Then there was the gym in Brooklyn, the bank, and last but not least, the spa in midtown. He pretty much gave them her whole life, but omitted her home address. They couldn't kill her at her house. Hassan would know who gave her up.

Next, Bimmy gave the country goons her license plate number and the make and model of the Benz she drove. Then finally, he removed an envelope from his jacket and handed it to Avery. In it was five grand, half the money now, the other half to be delivered when the job was done.

Avery happily took the cash and smiled.

"Don't fuck this up," Bimmy repeated sternly.

"We won't, cuz."

Bimmy took one last look at his hired killers and sighed. He then pivoted and left the room. He went down to his car and lingered behind the steering wheel for a moment. He wondered if he'd done the right thing, paying these thirsty fools half up front, and giving them the contract. Would they do the hit or take the money and run? Bimmy wouldn't lose a wink of sleep if forced to kill his own blood. But who had the time? He had too much shit going on.

As Bimmy continued to sit in his luxury vehicle, he thought about Pearla and wondered why he was going so hard. Why did he put his own life in danger just to kill her? He knew that if Hassan ever got wind of what was happening, he would be a dead man.

He lit a cigar and inhaled the taste. He exhaled, and once again thought about Pearla. At that moment, he admitted to himself that he was, in some strange way, jealous and angry. He felt betrayed when he saw Cash sneaking into her home that night. Secretly, he harbored feelings for her, but he could never act on them. She was a fine and beautiful woman. She was intelligent and independent. He thought about her constantly, and it stimulated him whenever she walked into the room. His blank stare never gave him away.

When Hassan got knocked, in the back of Bimmy's mind, there was hope. If Hassan got convicted for murder, then he could have made his move on Pearla. There was something about her that was too enticing. He wanted to fuck her. However, when he saw Cash, he felt deceived. To him, and most dudes who hustled hard, Cash was nothing but a pretty boy. That's it! He wasn't a real man—not a real hustler. He was soft—a bitch. His baby mama, April, was harder than Cash, Bimmy believed.

Now that he'd put out the hit, his gut was telling him to call it off, though his heart was telling him to put that bitch six feet deep. The wheels had started to turn, and everything had been set in motion. He wanted Cash's and Kwan's heads on a spike.

# TWENTY-TWO

Sophie paced around the living room trying to come up with the perfect plan to get Cash to speak to her. It had been months since she'd seen or heard from him. She was becoming desperate. Kwan was pushing her to contact him by any means necessary.

Sophia decided to change up tactics. She sighed heavily and then scooped up her cell phone from the bed and dialed Cash's number. His phone rang several times before her call was sent to voice mail, like always.

She left a message on his voice mail. "Cash, it's me again, Sophie. I know you're upset with me and you don't trust me, but we need to talk. It's really important. I'm pregnant, and it's your baby. And I'm sorry, baby. I miss you so much, and I love you. Please give me a call back." She hung up feeling that would get his attention. At least she hoped it did.

Her message was somewhat true. She was pregnant, but not by Cash. The baby belonged to some little nigga in Kwan's crew named Raymond. Sophie had started fucking him to get over Cash. He was a young cutie, tall and muscular, but no matter how many times he ran his dick inside of her, the nigga still couldn't compare to Cash. There was something about Cash that was unforgettable.

She missed Cash deeply, and in a strange way, she loved him. But under Kwan's pressure and influence, she wanted him dead too. Her brother was right—there was no coming back from his disrespect. She chose family over dick. And in her twisted mind, she felt that if she couldn't have him, then no one could. Not even that bitch Pearla.

\*\*\*

Cash stepped out of the shower and toweled off. He'd spent the past week cooped up in the motel room not doing much except working out, ordering Chinese food every day and watching TV. Then he'd call his contacts out in Brooklyn to get the 411 on what was happening and on his pops. Everything was cool with his pops, but Cash heard about Kwan killing one of Bimmy's men, a nigga named Run-Run. He didn't know the nigga and had never heard of him until his murder.

It wasn't surprising to him that Kwan got to someone close to Bimmy. It was his nature. He was a monster.

The war would only escalate. Neither side would stop. The bloodshed would continue until the entire city was covered in blood. Cash wanted to be as far away from that as possible. He still thought about leaving town and starting over somewhere. He had enough money on him to live anywhere. The drug game and stealing cars had been good to him. He had profited greatly from both illegal ventures and had the cash to become a new man. It wasn't in the millions, but it was enough money for a house and a new life in a different state.

He wrapped the towel around his waist and walked out of the bathroom. Of course, he had his guns out, the shades were drawn, and the bolt lock was across the door. Like routine, he started his workout, a few calisthenics to shape his body. He did fifty push-ups and a hundred sit-ups, and worked on his biceps and triceps. To Cash, his body was the most important thing to him. He needed to stay fit and strong. The motel room became his private gym.

After his forty-minute workout, he wiped the sweat from his hard-looking body and downed some bottled water. Working out kept him busy and focused.

He realized he hadn't had sex in several weeks. It was a first for him, going without sex for so long. His energy was up. He was animated and alive. He looked at himself in the mirror and liked what he saw. He was still young and handsome, and he didn't want to die. He was just too handsome to die.

Looking down at the bed, Cash saw that he had a few missed calls. He picked it up, scrolled down his missed call list and saw that Sophie had called him once again and left another message. At first, he wanted to delete it, but he decided against it and listened to the voice message she'd left on his phone. Cash listened to her message stating that she was pregnant by him. Automatically he felt that it was only a ruse to get his attention and have him call her back. She sounded sincere in the message, but he didn't believe her.

Anyway, he decided to call her back. Not because she was pregnant, but because he did need her help. He had been avoiding her for too long, and he needed her help to call off the dogs. If anyone could stop Kwan from murdering him, it probably would be Sophie. Just as he asked Pearla to call off Hassan, he was going to ask Sophie to do the same thing. He felt that she had some influence over her brother.

Cash was desperate to bring peace, somehow, some way. He was tired of the bullshit. Overnight, he'd had an epiphany. He strongly felt that there was something out there better for him. Someplace far away from New York—a new life, hope, and a different bitch. And when he left, he didn't want to be looking over his shoulders. He knew that one day Kwan, or Bimmy, and Hassan would kill each other, but what would stop the last man standing from coming after him?

Though Cash was a free man, he felt imprisoned by concern and the sins of his past. A year from now, when he was living his life comfortably, who was to say someone wouldn't recognize him and put a bullet in the back of his head because they hadn't forgotten about the past?

He had to do something. If he had to swallow his pride and make amends to some dangerous men and bitches, then so be it. He wasn't going to continue to cower and hide in some motel room. He had to take a risk either with war or making peace.

Sophie's phone rang twice before she picked up. "Hello?" she sounded eager to speak.

"It's me. You really pregnant?" Cash asked, not beating around the bush.

"I am. Five months."

So far the time frame added up. But he didn't trust her.

"I miss you, Cash. I really do. Where are you?"

Cash refused to answer the question. There was no way in hell he was about to give up his location. "I'm somewhere," he replied, being short.

"It's good to hear your voice again, baby. I'm sorry for everything."

"Where's your brother?" he asked.

"I have no idea. We haven't spoken to each other in months," she lied.

"Why not?"

"Because of you. He's still out for blood, Cash, and he wants your head on a platter. But I stood up for you. I told him that you're the father of my unborn baby and I wasn't goin' to help him kill you. No matter what you think about me, Cash, I'm still in love with you."

Cash wasn't buying her story. There was something off. Kwan and Sophie had always been close, and she loved her brother greatly. There was no way they would have a falling out over him. He was the one who cheated. He was the one who betrayed them by warning Pearla. It didn't make any sense, but he continued to entertain her.

"Do you know what you're havin'?"

"I'm having a boy. You're gonna have a son."

"A son, huh?"

"Yes. Are you excited?"

Cash walked toward the window and took a quick peek outside. It had become a routine thing for him—always checking, always being observant.

"I wanna see you, Cash. Please!" she said. "I just want you to come home. I want us to be a family."

"A family?"

"Yes."

"So we supposed to become the Brady Bunch overnight, after everything that's happened, and wit' your brother looking to kill me?"

"I know it's crazy right now, but everything is gonna work itself out. You'll see."

"How?" he asked.

"Let me see you, and we'll talk. I promise you, it will only be you and me, nobody else."

Cash was leery of a face-to-face with her. He didn't believe he could ever have a family with her. The sex with her was good—great actually—but he never did see a future with Sophie. It was fun while it lasted.

"I can talk to Kwan, and I'll get him to see things my way. You know I can, Cash. I'll get him to squash the beef he has wit' you."

It sounded sweet, but Cash was still hesitant to meet up with her.

"Besides, I have some information that you might want to have."

"What kind of information?"

"I'm not gonna discuss it over the phone. You'll have to meet me somewhere."

Cash heaved a sigh, and then he relented. "Okay, I'll meet you. It's gotta be in public and during the day."

Sophie smiled. "Wherever is comfortable for you, baby."

"The Starbucks in downtown Brooklyn. Meet me there at noon tomorrow," he said.

Sophie agreed.

Cash felt comfortable meeting Sophie at a Starbucks in downtown Brooklyn. One, there would be hordes of people around. Two, there would be police; they were a heavy presence downtown. Three, he knew the area well. They would have to be stupid and crazy to try anything in that area with so many witnesses, traffic, and police. He was going to ready himself. He wasn't about to be a fool and walk into a trap. No way.

# TWENTY-THREE

Downtown Brooklyn was a busy area jumbled with office and residential buildings, traffic, people, and stores. The Starbucks on Fulton Street was the perfect location for Cash to meet with Sophie, being one of the busier stores around, with constant traffic flowing and the NYPD ever present.

Cash made sure to arrive at the location a few hours before noon. It was still early, and the crowd wasn't so thick. He parked his Lexus in the nearest garage and walked the streets armed with a neatly concealed .9mm. He was disguised, looking unassuming in a snug-fit beanie, dark glasses, heavy book bag, and a John Jay hoodie. He looked like one of the many college students that patronized the shops and stores in the area.

Cash went into the Burger King across the street, ordered something simple, and went to the second floor of the fast-food establishment. He took a window seat, one that overlooked everything below, including the front entrance of the Starbucks across the street.

Cash didn't mind hanging out and staking out the place. He nibbled at his small order and took up time just chilling and watching everything around him. He had to be extra cautious. There was no telling who was watching the area too. But Kwan was never one for subtlety and patience.

Around a quarter to ten, Cash saw Sophie and her brother Kwan get out of a Yukon. Sophie was pregnant; Cash could see that from a mile away. Kwan had also brought a few of his goons with him. They were over two hours early, thinking they were going to have the jump on him.

Cash frowned. Sophie was trying to set him up again. He knew it. It was all a lie. He shook his head, knowing he had good reason not to trust that bitch. He lifted himself up from the table and made his exit quietly. He was furious—both his bitches didn't give a fuck about him. He had to do it by himself.

He said to himself, *What did I ever do wrong?* He had tried making peace, but there was no way around it. He had to get ready for war.

# TWENTY-FOUR

Perez couldn't believe his luck. Due to improper procedures during the grand jury hearing and an error on the prosecution's part, the judge dropped all of the charges against him. He was a free man. He had a second chance at life. Now he had a second chance to kill Cash and Pearla with his own free hands. He couldn't wait. He was thirsting for it. He knew that sometimes if you want something done right, then you have to do it yourself.

He lingered in the dayroom thinking about his release the following day. He stood alone, minding his business. He stayed his distance from Hassan. His last meeting with the man had been a disaster. It was no use trying to get Hassan to do his dirty work; the man was too smart for that.

Hassan was holding court in the dayroom with his crew. No one dared to bother them, not even the guards. Perez watched them from a safe distance. He didn't want any dealings with Hassan or his cronies. They already thought he was a jailhouse snitch. So he turned and went the opposite direction. Today would be his last day in this hellhole. Good riddance!

Leaving the dayroom, one of Hassan's young goons deliberately bumped into him and then stared him down like he was in the wrong. "Nigga, you forgot how to walk? Watch where you going!"

Perez glared at him. He didn't say a word.

"You out tomorrow, huh, nigga. Have fun, and Hassan says hi," the kid said.

Perez didn't respond. They were only trying to push his buttons. He was going home. He didn't have to worry about Rikers Island anymore. Leaving the room, Perez noticed Hassan watching him, and he wondered what that was about. He shrugged it off and left.

✳✳✳

The following day, the paperwork for his release was processed, and Perez stepped out of Rikers Island jail a free and happy man. He looked up at the sky and smiled. *God is good,* he thought to himself.

He boarded the next bus leaving the island and took a seat by the window. He exhaled, like Whitney, and looked at the people getting on the bus too. Two other inmates were also released, one older man and a younger female. Besides the three of them, the bus was packed with visitors leaving the island after their hour visit with loved ones.

The bus crossed the bridge, and Perez got off at its first stop with only a few belongings on him. After the bus drove off, Perez saw his friend Monica standing by her white Lexus waiting for him in the parking lot. She smiled at him, and he smiled back. He hurried her way, and they hugged each other warmly.

"I'm home, baby!" he announced excitedly.

"I know they couldn't keep you," she said.

"You know it."

Perez took a step back and stared at Monica dressed in a pair of tight denim jeans that accentuated her hips, high heels, and a black shawl. Her Puerto Rican complexion glimmered in the sunlight, and her long black hair was flowing in the light wind.

"You look nice," he said.

She smiled.

"Let's get the fuck outta here. I had enough of this place," he said.

She was about to get into the driver's side, but Perez said, "Nah, baby, I'll drive. I need you to keep busy with something else for me."

She tossed him the keys and smiled. She knew what he meant.

He slid behind the wheel, and she rode shotgun. Perez thought he would never be behind the wheel of a car again. He'd thought he would never be back home. But he was, and he planned on taking full advantage.

Perez steered Monica's Lexus out of the jail parking lot and headed toward the highway. The moment he got onto the Grand Central Parkway, Monica leaned into his lap and unzipped his pants. She pulled out his dick and wrapped her full, glossy lips around it and started sucking him off.

He moaned while keeping full control of the car. It had been a while since he'd enjoyed the feel of a woman. He needed something to help him escape for the moment, and a blowjob was the perfect remedy.

Monica stroked his hard dick and worked his mushroom tip with her long tongue.

"Oh shit! Damn! That feels good, baby," he moaned. "I'm never gonna get locked up again. I missed this."

Monica's head bobbed up and down with Perez's dick down her throat as he did sixty on the parkway. He was going back to his old neighborhood to connect with his crew and some old friends. He had a lot to get back. He'd lost his chop shop and his business connects, and that was going to take some time to recover. But he was determined. Cash had ruined him, he felt, and now it was time to return the favor.

Perez had one hand around the steering wheel and the other hand moving through Monica's hair as she continued sucking his dick. She was a sexy and beautiful woman, and Perez felt blessed that she was there for him. She had been there for him since day one, sexually and emotionally.

Monica was focused on pleasing him, wanting him to bust a nut while driving. Not once did she come up for air or to look around.

"Oh shit! I'm gonna come!"

Her mouth and tongue went into overdrive. Her lips were like a vacuum as she tried to milk the come from his balls. Her lips squeezed around his dick tighter, moving up and down, her tongue wrapped around his erection like a coiled snake. The rapid motion was mind-blowing.

Perez came so hard, his sperm shot to the back of Monica's throat. Monica didn't budge. She swallowed every ounce of him without flinching at all. Surprisingly, Perez still kept control of the car on the highway. He didn't even swerve.

Monica propped herself back up in the front seat and wiped her mouth. Perez had the biggest smile on his face. It was his welcome-home gift. Now that he'd had his sexual healing, it was time to get back to business.

The old neighborhood welcomed Perez with open arms when he climbed out of the Lexus with Monica by his side. His old crew, excited to see him back on the block, surrounded him with hugs and daps.

Perez looked around and took it all in. When he was home and had things up and running, everybody was getting money. They loved him. He was the source of income to many of the folks on the block. He was fair, and he was cool. Then, because of a certain snitch, it all came to an end. He was down, but he wasn't out.

There was plenty to do. First thing, revenge—kill Cash and Pearla. He knew that bitch was with Hassan now, so the hit on her had to be subtle.

Next, get another chop shop up and running. He needed to reach out to his old sources and let everyone know he was back home now. He'd stood tall while locked down. He told on no one and kept his head up. Everyone had to respect him for that.

"Welcome home, Perez."

"It's good to see you back."

"Yo, we ready to get this money again."

"I missed you."

"Yo, we ready to ride wit' you, my nigga!"

Perez was getting love from everyone. Without him, the hood wasn't the same. He smiled. He felt that he was in a really good place. These were his peoples. They took care of him, and he took care of them.

He looked at Monica and smiled at her. Though she was never his girlfriend, she had always been there for him too. He couldn't wait to finish what they'd started in the car. He was hungry for some pussy. She was the one. He was ready to throw her legs back and pound away.

The Brooklyn block was live. Some people were ready to start barbecuing on the street to make Perez's homecoming a party. He was ready to celebrate and socialize, but first he wanted to shower and change clothes to wash away that jail scent.

Perez felt like he had nothing to worry about in his neighborhood as he and Monica walked toward her building, talking and laughing. He felt human again. So when the burgundy minivan with the tinted windows drove his way, he didn't seem concerned at all. It was just another passing vehicle on the street.

Then suddenly the side doors flew open, and several armed gunmen jumped out of the minivan with automatic weapons and opened fire at him. Quickly, he and Monica took cover as bullets went flying by their heads, shattering car windows and piercing everything around them. The gunfire was loud and chaotic. They rushed toward him with one intent—murder!

"Oh shit! Yo, they tryin' to kill Perez," someone from his crew shouted.

More guns were pulled out, and a heated gunfight took place. Bullets went flying everywhere. People in the area quickly ran away and frantically took cover. Just like that, things went from a joyous event to the O.K. Corral. It was war on the block.

Then, just like that, the shooting was over. The men in the van jumped inside the van and sped off as a few bullets shattered the back window, but inside no one was hit.

When the gunfire ceased and the smoke cleared, Monica was screaming her head off. Perez was dead. He had been gunned down—a bullet in his head and one in his chest. She cradled his body in her arms and screamed in agony.

His crew looked down at his body in disbelief. They were angry. He had just come home. How and why did it happen? Who sent the goons? It could have been anyone. But on top of the list was either Hassan or Cash.

# TWENTY-FIVE

With Cash acting like a pussy and a spineless fruitcake all of a sudden and Hassan locked up, Pearla hadn't had sex in a while. Her body was yearning for it. So she had purchased a few sex toys and put them to use in the privacy of her bedroom.

After drinking a half bottle of red wine, listening to some slow jams, and thinking about a few past lovers, she found herself wound up with lust. She had all the money she needed, thanks to Hassan, but she had no man to lie next to her, comfort her, and fuck her right. She had no friends. She felt alone. In the late evening, the only friend she had was her vibrator.

Sprawled on her back with her legs spread, she put the vibrator against her clit. She moaned pleasingly. Her body heaved up and down. She closed her eyes and enjoyed the AAA batteries that were bringing her toy to life, along with her clit and pussy.

She let out a loud moan as she felt her buildup. She worked the toy against her clit like it was magic. Her legs quivered with anticipation. She closed her eyes and whined louder, almost sounding like a siren. The sensation was taking her to a whole new place.

*Fuck everyone!* she thought. *Who needs a man?* In today's world, a good toy could please a woman just as well. But who was she fooling? She missed Cash's long, deep strokes inside of her, his touch, and his kisses. Yes, a sex toy could please her and make her come, but it couldn't hold her afterwards. It couldn't speak and comfort her. It couldn't give her reassurance and good company.

Pearla needed to come. She needed some kind of pleasure in her life. She focused on her clit the most. The way the machine beat against her private spot, it was a wonder she didn't take off and hit the ceiling. The walls of the bedroom absorbed her loud, passionate cries, and the dimmed light hid her naughtiness.

Little beads of sweat covered her body. The muscles in her pussy were flexing. Her nipples were hard, and her flesh was burning up with a sensational orgasm approaching between her legs. She wanted to forget about the selfish prick, but the closer she came to orgasm, the more she thought about him. Why was she thinking about him? She had cursed him out at the motel. She finally saw his selfish ways and wasn't blinded by him anymore. She had on her dark shades and turned her gaze away from the sun. But yet, there he was, his handsome image creeping into her mind while she masturbated and fingered herself and her vibrant machine was going into overdrive with her clit.

Her chest heaved up and down rapidly. It was coming. She squirmed across her beige satin sheets. "Aaaah! Aaaah! Oh shit! Ooooh!" the sound spilled from her mouth like heated liquid. She exploded alone inside the bedroom and couldn't help but to call out his name. "Oh, Cash!"

When her orgasm was over, and she finally came to her senses, Pearla cursed herself for thinking about that fool while she was playing with her pussy. He didn't deserve her time.

She picked herself up from the bed and exhaled. Her naked body was still feeling the aftereffects from the toy. She went on trying to collect herself, but the moment she did, the doorbell sounded.

It was late in the evening, and she wasn't expecting company. She wondered who it could be. She donned her long robe and went to the door. Peeking outside, she saw it was Bimmy. She grimaced. She wasn't in the mood to deal with him, but she had no choice. The nigga was Hassan's errand boy, and maybe he had some important news to tell her. Pearla made sure her robe was securely tied before she opened the door.

Bimmy walked in.

She said, "Wow! He rings the doorbell this time."

Bimmy didn't respond to her comment.

"Why are you here, Bimmy?" Pearla kept a reasonable distance from him. The man gave her the chills. She would look into his eyes and felt that he was up to no good most times.

He looked her up and down. "I just wanted to let you know, that fool Perez is dead," he said.

"Perez?" She barely remembered the name, but then it dawned on her that he was the fool she and Cash had scammed some serious money from.

"And you came to my door to tell me this?"

"I thought you might want to hear the news in person."

She sighed. "Really? I don't care for him or you right now in my home."

"I understand."

"What else are you here for, Bimmy?" Pearla asked impolitely.

"I'm just checking up on you, making sure you're okay."

"I'm fine. So unless you have something to tell me about Hassan, or have some money for me, I would appreciate if you leave my house."

The way he looked at her, she could feel the nigga's eyes judging.

"How's April?" Pearla asked out of the blue, since he wasn't rushing to exit her home.

"She's fine."

"Give her my love."

Bimmy didn't say anything back. He simply stood there looking at her coldly. Pearla wondered if he was dumb enough to try anything with her. Hassan would kill him.

"Have you seen Cash lately?" he asked out of the blue.

Pearla was caught off-guard hearing Cash's name come out of his mouth. "Cash? Why you askin' about him? I haven't seen that fool in a while," she lied.

Once again, Bimmy's hard and cold stare fell on her, making it feel like an Antarctic night inside her living room. Now she was worried. Did Bimmy know about them? Had he seen her with Cash recently? Was he there to kill her? So many horrible things flooded her head.

"I'm just asking, that's all," he said. "I know the two of y'all were very close not too long ago."

"Well, you're askin' the wrong fuckin' person. I don't give a fuck about Cash, and I don't know where that nigga is at! He can burn in hell for all I care."

Bimmy nodded. "Well, just watch your back. You know there's a war out there."

"I know. I keep my ear to the streets."

Pearla knew he was trying to feel her out. Maybe he thought that by bringing up Cash's name, she would suddenly get nervous and fidgety around him. She didn't. She stood tall and firm. She didn't budge or break.

"You done, nigga?" she asked gruffly.

He smirked. Then he replied, "Yeah, I'm done. Just be careful."

"I will. Bye!" Pearla had her hands on her hips and an attitude across her face.

Bimmy turned and left her home, and Pearla slammed the door behind him, securing every lock. She knew something was up, but she couldn't figure out exactly what. Bimmy knew something, but he wasn't revealing his cards yet.

Pearla exhaled and leaned against the door. *Damn! Did he see me with Cash or not?* She was experiencing an intense feeling of worry and guilt. *What kind of game is this nigga playing?*

She couldn't dwell on Bimmy. She had a life to live and a plan to implement. She was still putting money away in her safe deposit box, still being careful everywhere she went, and she always carried her pistol with her.

Every time Bimmy came around her, she always felt the need to take a shower. And that's what she did. She peeled off her robe and stepped into the warm shower to cleanse herself of any guilt and dirt.

While in the shower, she thought of the one person she needed to see—April. She needed to have a one-on-one girl talk with her. If anyone had a clue what was going on with Bimmy and everything else, Pearla was sure that April knew. Bimmy rarely hid anything from her.

# TWENTY-SIX

A green Cherokee came to a stop in front of the local bodega on Mother Gaston Boulevard. A young man sat behind the wheel of the Jeep next to a beautiful Latino woman with long, jet-black hair and a curvy, luscious figure. Rap music blared from the sound system. It was late evening, and the streets were crawling with people and traffic. The young man, dressed in a Yankees ball cap, a white T-shirt, gold chain with a diamond cross hanging from around his neck, and sagging jeans was all laughter and smiles with his female companion. He was a player on the streets and a drug dealer with heavy status in Kwan's crew. His name was Butter, and his skin complexion was just like that, butter.

Butter took a pull from the cigarette in his hand and nodded to the rap music, his .380 concealed underneath the driver's seat.

"Yo, ma, you want anything from the store?" he asked the girl.

"Yeah, get me a pack of cigarettes since you smoked all of mines."

He laughed. "Oh, my bad! I got you, though, wit' ya sexy ass." He placed his hand on her thigh and rubbed it.

She didn't budge. The smile she gave back to him indicated that she was ready to play too. "You better not start somethin' that you ain't gonna finish," she said with a playful smile.

"Oh, you know I always finish what I started. You ain't even gotta worry 'bout that, ma. You ain't fuckin' wit no weak nigga right here."

"We'll see." She continued to smile.

Butter took one last drag from the cigarette and flicked it out the window. Hard like a brick, he was anxious to take the thick Latina beauty back to his place on Blake Avenue. He had plans for that sweet, round ass. He removed himself from his jeep and walked into the bodega.

The female friend remained seated in the passenger seat and checked her hair and makeup in the sun visor. She was ready to give Butter the best time of his life. She had on a skirt with no panties. She was a gold-digger and knew Butter was a nigga with some money. She only fucked with drug dealers and hustlers, nothing less.

"He better not take forever," she said to herself.

Five minutes later, Butter walked out of the bodega with a plastic bag full of stuff, including her cigarettes and Magnum condoms. He was all smiles. As he walked toward his truck, he didn't see the two masked men coming, both armed and in all black.

They rushed toward him with Glock 17s in their hands, outstretched their arms, and aimed at him. They didn't hesitate to fire. *Boom! Boom! Boom! Boom! Boom! Boom! Boom!*

The gunmen drilled seven bullets into Butter's body, and he died on the spot. His body slumped, and a pool of blood started to seep out from under the fallen thug.

His female friend in the passenger seat started to scream frantically. She couldn't believe what she had just witnessed.

One of the gunmen hurried her way and shouted, "Shut the fuck up, bitch!" and the sound of more gunfire followed. *Boom! Boom!* He put two into her head, leaving her slumped in the seat.

The gunmen hurried off, leaving behind many stunned and horrified witnesses. It was revenge for Run-Run's murder, and there was more to come.

*** 

Two days later, there were three more shootings in the Brownsville area, and another one of Kwan's men was viciously gunned down as he waited inside the Chinese restaurant for his takeout. They put eight bullets into his head and tore his face apart. The NYPD, especially in the Brooklyn area, were becoming overwhelmed with so many homicides.

It was starting to look like *The War of the Worlds* in one New York City ghetto.

# TWENTY-SEVEN

Pearla parked her Benz on the Manhattan street on a beautiful, sunny fall day and stepped out looking fabulous, all the while showing off every one of her curves in the black jumpsuit featuring side cutouts, a V-neckline, and body-conscious fabric. She strutted toward the hair salon carrying her clutch bag, her Louboutins click-clacking on the city pavement.

Once again, Hassan had supplied her with some money: fifteen grand to take care of the bills and to take care of her needs. Pearla wanted to get her hair done and spend the day pampering herself. She wanted it to be a stress-free day.

She walked into the high-end salon expecting her beautician to be around, but to her shock, Melinda wasn't there today. Pearla was disappointed. Melinda was the best in the city and the only one she trusted with her hair.

Pearla sighed with displeasure, pivoted in her Louboutins, and walked right back out of the salon. She strutted toward her Benz, slid her sexy ass behind the wheel, and started the car. She shifted the car into drive and accelerated moderately.

Unbeknownst to Pearla, she was being watched and followed by Avery and Dalou. They had a tail on her and were ready to strike when the time was right. They believed that second five thousand dollars was almost in their hands, and they were ready to party and become legit gangsters in the eyes of Bimmy.

*** 

The next morning, Pearla got up at the crack of dawn, dressed nicely in a pair of tight jeans and a peach top, got into her Benz, and made her way to Brooklyn. She remembered where April used to take her kids to day care. She was planning to surprise her. She drove a good distance to the day care and arrived just in time to see numerous parents dropping off their children.

Pearla stayed parked across the street and watched every car come to a stop and every parent escort their little ones into the two-story building in Bay Ridge, Brooklyn, a largely middle-class neighborhood with a strong family presence and a sizable population of Italian, Greek, and Irish heritage. The area didn't surprise Pearla. She knew April always wanted the best for her kids, and the day care was one of the best in the city.

After waiting ten minutes, Pearla stared at the black GLK-Class Benz pulling up to the day care. She had an idea who was driving the truck. As predicted, April stepped out looking suave in a pair of Soho jeans and a classy burgundy button-down top underneath a pumpkin-colored fall leather jacket and walked into the day care with her three kids.

Pearla got out of her car and casually walked toward the entrance. She waited for April to come back out.

Five minutes later, the front door opened, and April strutted out of the building, kid-free. She walked toward her truck, not knowing that she was being watched. She hit the alarm button, and before she could take another step forward, Pearla called out to her.

"April!"

April spun around quickly and was taken aback by Pearla just showing up out of the blue. "What the fuck you doin' here, Pearla?"

"I just came to see you to talk," Pearla explained.

April raised an eyebrow. "Talk?"

She stood in front of Pearla looking skeptical. She didn't have her gun on her. She cursed herself for being so sloppy. But April started to relax, trying not to become too paranoid. "What the fuck you wanna talk about, Pearla? Huh?"

"Why are you isolating me, April? What did I do to you? Can you at least give me an explanation? The only thing I ever did was try to be your friend."

Pearla wasn't allowing April out of her sight until she got some answers from her. She was determined to get back on her good side.

"Friend?" April laughed.

"Yes, friend! I thought we were cool, April. You and I, we had each other's back."

"We had each other's back—key word, Pearla, *had*." April shot back. "And I barely knew you."

"Look, I just wanna talk to you and let bygones be bygones. Let me take you out to eat. My treat."

April sighed. Her hard stare at Pearla began to subside. She didn't mind a free food on Pearla. "Fuck it! But don't play me, bitch."

"April, I know how you get down, and believe me, it didn't even cross my mind. I just want to talk, that's all."

Pearla got behind the wheel of her Benz, and April jumped into her Benz truck and followed her. So far, so good. Pearla knew the perfect place for them to sit down and enjoy a meal together.

The River Café on Water Street in downtown Brooklyn was an eclectic place with a stunning view of the Brooklyn Bridge and the Manhattan skyline. There, they cooked in a classical French cuisine tradition. The ladies sat across from each other and mingled in with the morning crowd coming from all areas of downtown Brooklyn.

Pearla and April ordered the French toast, omelets, turkey sausages, and Bloody Mary's.

After downing her first cocktail, April decided to spill it. She and Pearla came there to talk woman to woman. Though Pearla had initiated the conversation, it didn't make any sense for her to beat around the bush.

Pearla looked at April harmlessly.

April looked back with an awkward stare. "You came here to talk about you and Cash, right, bitch?"

Pearla was floored. Her mouth flew open. "What?"

"Oh, don't bullshit me, Pearla! I know your reason for having this lunch wit' me. My man suspects that you fuckin' wit' that nigga Cash. And what, bitch? You came to get information from me, huh?"

Pearla quickly denied it. "Why would he think I'm dealing with my ex? I'm not!"

"Because you are a grimy, backstabbing bitch!"

"You think I'm a backstabbing bitch?"

"I only call 'em like I see 'em," April said. "Hassan has been really good to you, and you do him dirty by goin' around and fuckin' wit' that nigga."

"I love Hassan."

"You sure 'bout that? Because you definitely have a funny way of showing it."

"First off, you got the wrong information. I haven't seen Cash in months, and Bimmy needs to get his facts right."

"So you tryin' to call my man a liar?"

"What proof does he have?"

April exclaimed. "Plenty!"

"Well, he can't take his plenty and shove it somewhere dark and nasty, because I've been truly faithful to Hassan. You don't know shit, and he sure doesn't know shit about me!"

Though she was going back and forth with April to protect her lie, Pearla was really scared. Surely, if April knew, that meant Hassan knew, and her life could be in danger. But if Hassan knew, then why was she still alive? Why didn't he react? Every visit to Rikers, everything between them was copacetic and loving.

"You talkin' all that shit now, Pearla."

"I don't need to talk shit, because I'm talking the truth."

"I thought you were a real bitch," April said.

"I am a real bitch," Pearla came back, holding down a staring contest with April. "Don't fuckin' get me twisted!"

April was protecting her man's word and reputation tooth and nail. But she didn't know about Bimmy's plan to have Pearla murdered without Hassan's consent.

"So if you're not fuckin' around on Hassan, then tell me this—Why he saw Cash go inside your crib one night and he didn't come right back out?"

Pearla's heart dropped into her stomach. She felt like she was caught red-handed, but she refused to go down like the Titanic. Her ship wasn't sinking yet, but if it was, she had an escape plan. She had money saved, a passport and driver's license in a different name in her safety deposit box, and a few faraway places to escape to.

"You sit here and fuckin' judge me, April, like you a saint."

"Bitch, I'm not judging you."

"You could have fooled me. So what now?" Pearla asked boldly.

"What you mean?"

Pearla looked at her intently. "You gonna shoot me because you think I'm cheatin' on Hassan?"

"Relax, bitch."

"What? You wanna fuck my man? Huh?"

April warned, "Bitch, don't you dare get outta fuckin' line wit' me."

"I'm not gonna sit here and be disrespected, April."

April chuckled. "You are a trip, Pearla. Like I said, you need to fuckin' relax."

"How you gonna tell me to relax?"

"Because I can. You need to get you another cocktail and watch how the fuck you talkin' to me."

Pearla frowned. She felt like she was being forced into a situation that was going to lead to her doom. There was no way she was going to directly confess to having sex with her ex-boyfriend. It was insane.

However, maybe there was still some hope. Pearla was a smart woman. She knew how to talk and influence people. She felt that if April was totally against her, then she wouldn't have had lunch with her.

"I just want us to be cool, April," she said civilly.

"Just don't lie to me, ho."

"I'm not."

April finished off the rest of her cocktail and then ordered another one. She then said to Pearla, "Bitch, it's your pussy, and you can do with it what you please. You want the truth—I myself have crept out on Bimmy and fucked a few niggas here and there. We ain't fuckin' perfect, right? I'm not gonna fuckin' lie. You got yourself a good man in Hassan, and you better keep that nigga around for your benefit. I'm just sayin' to you that shit is out there, bitch, and you're fuckin' sloppy wit' it. Hassan is my friend. So you can deny it all you want, but I'm gonna protect his best interest."

Pearla was confused as fuck. She had no idea what that bitch was talking about. She wanted to tell April how Bimmy was up in her place, chilling in her bedroom when she had just come out of the shower, that she had noticed how he had been looking at her lately, but she decided against it. There was too much shit going on at the moment. There was no need to add the extra drama.

After dining on a perfectly cooked breakfast and sipping on a few more cocktails, the tension between April and Pearla cooled down. Before they knew it, they were chatting it up like old, drunken friends.

After brunch and several cocktails, April wanted to get blunted before she picked up her kids. "Bitch, let's go to my cousin's place and get some weed. He got the best shit in the city."

Pearla agreed. She needed to get high right now. She needed to run away from her troubles. She was happy that everything with April went well.

As they walked to their cars, Pearla pulled out her car keys. April immediately snatched them from out her hands and said, "Bitch, I'll drive your shit. Ain't no sense in us takin' two fuckin' cars to the projects, and my ride is low on gas."

Pearla didn't mind. "Let's go then."

April jumped into the driver's seat, and Pearla sat in the passenger seat. A sudden calm came over Pearla as April drove them to see her cousin Ricky, a weed dealer in the Van Dyke houses in Brownsville.

\*\*\*

Since Bimmy had given Avery and Dalou the five grand, they went crazy spending it on drugs, booze, and whores. Every day was a party in their motel room. After smoking and drinking, they got down to business—following Pearla around—but barely doing a good job at that.

Sky high on weed laced with cocaine, their eyes glossy and bloodshot, they had been following Pearla all morning, from place to place, leading them to the River Café. Dalou started the car and continued to trail Pearla's Benz in Brooklyn.

The men were so high, they didn't realize that Pearla wasn't driving her own car.

# TWENTY-EIGHT

April navigated Pearla's Benz to the Van Dyke Houses on Blake Avenue, a sprawling twenty-two-building complex bordered by Mother Gaston Boulevard, Powell Street, Sutter Avenue, and Livonia Avenue. The day was still young, and that meant people roaming around everywhere.

April parked the Benz right across the street from the projects, looked at Pearla and said, "Give me ten minutes. We gonna get high today." She hopped out of the car and went into the projects.

Pearla just sat back and chilled. She reclined in the seat and pulled out her smartphone to peruse Twitter while waiting for April to come back out with the bomb weed from her cousin Ricky.

After that, she did the unthinkable. She called Cash, but he didn't answer. His phone went directly to his voice mail. She left a message: "You need to call me back, ASAP!"

She waited a few minutes, and Cash still didn't call her back. She sighed. She needed to speak to him and give him the heads-up. So she decided to text him. The last thing she needed was for Cash to call while she was with April. She texted: HASSAN AND BIMMY KNOW ABOUT US. DON'T CALL! I'LL FILL U IN L8TER!

Right after sending her text message to Cash, Pearla saw April leaving the project building and walking back to the car with a long smile on her face. So many things were going through her head. Could she trust April enough to get high with her? Was this part of a ruse? She did relent easily, and now it appeared that they were best friends again. But what about Bimmy? As far as Pearla knew, it all could be a ploy to get her to let her guard down and then *bang!*—She gets fucked! She released a temper sigh. Now she was having second thoughts.

Parked nearby were Avery and Dalou, with Dalou in the driver's seat as the getaway driver.

Avery, high like a kite, followed April with his gun in hand. He moved briskly her way, and when he got close enough to her, he raised the gun to the back of her head and fired without an ounce of hesitation. *Bak! Bak! Bak!*

The bullets pushed her body forward violently, and immediately, April fell to the concrete, where she died on the spot.

Before anyone could process what had happened, Avery was sprinting back to the car. He leaped inside, and Dalou took off like he was a driver in the Indy 500.

Pearla looked at the murder in disbelief. Her mouth was open like she was about to scream, but nothing came out. She was in utter shock. It seemed like a nightmare. There was no way April had just been shot. Nah, that was Bimmy's baby mama. What fools had the overconfidence to pull off such a suicide mission?

The people in the area were caught off guard by the gunfire too. It happened so fast. A few had seen the shooter flee from the scene on foot and get into a Ford Focus. They ran toward the body, which lay face down, and saw two holes in the back of her head and one in her neck.

\*\*\*

Bimmy sat in a black Escalade in the parking lot of Rikers Island. He was smoking a cigar whilst he waited patiently for Hassan's release.

He couldn't believe it. The nigga actually pulled it off. He got Lamiek to confess to all the felony charges. The young nigga ate the gun and murder charges like soul food. Of course, he had no choice, since Hassan had offered him a deal he couldn't refuse.

The prosecution went haywire. They didn't know what to do with themselves. They wanted Hassan to remain in jail, being the drug kingpin and more of a threat on the streets. But his lawyers were the best, and they were adamant in pushing for his release. Hassan played chess with the system and hit checkmate with his case.

Hassan was taken to the male booking area, where he signed his release papers. He was given the street clothes he was arrested in and was allowed to dress out. After a half-hour process, he was taken downstairs, his personal items in hand, and was able to walk out of the jail. Hassan wanted everything to be hush-hush. The only people who knew he was coming home were Bimmy, his lawyer, and Lamiek. Also, he wanted to sneak up on Pearla and finally get to the bottom of things. He certainly had unfinished business with Cash, Kwan, and some other ignorant goons that weren't loyal to his organization.

Bimmy was on edge as he waited. The man was coming home today, and yet Pearla was still alive. He started to regret hiring them two fools to pull off the job. He frowned with a fire stirring inside of his belly. For certain, after his business with Hassan was done, he was going to the motel Avery and Dalou were in and raise hell. He wanted all of his money back, and if those two fools spent it, then they were dead men.

Just then, his cell phone rang. It was Avery calling. He answered right away, hoping against hope. "What, nigga?" he answered roughly.

"It's done," Avery said.

Bimmy couldn't believe his ears. He was sorry that he'd doubted them, and that he had thought about killing his own cousin. "Okay, y'all niggas just sit tight and chill," he said. "I'll bring what I owe tonight."

He hung up. He didn't want to say too much over the phone, especially a cell phone. He felt a huge sigh of relief. Finally! Now that Pearla was gone, his boss should be able to think straight again.

He sat practicing his facial expression in the sun visor. How should he react once news got out about Pearla? He didn't want to underplay or overplay the scene and make Hassan suspicious.

Fifteen minutes passed, and Bimmy felt he had his reaction down pat. He got out of the truck and stood watch for Hassan's arrival. His phone rang again. He already knew the deal. People were calling him to tell him Pearla had been murdered. He didn't know the details yet, but he needed to wait until he was with Hassan, so his reaction could be more authentic.

Hassan stepped off the city bus casually and saw Bimmy posted up against the truck waiting for him. Hassan walked his way.

Bimmy was feeling ambivalent about his friend's sudden release. The shit was about to hit the fan and spread everywhere. He took a deep breath and greeted Hassan with a dap and a brotherly hug. "Welcome home, my nigga," he said.

"It's good to be out finally!" Hassan exclaimed. The man was hyped and ready to carry on with business as usual. He climbed into the passenger seat of the truck and was already on a mission. "Yo, take me straight to see Pearla. I wanna surprise my bitch," he said.

Bimmy nodded his head as he drove away from the jail. He offered Hassan a cell phone. "You wanna call her now?"

"Nah, I came this far, and I definitely want to see the look on her face when she sees I'm out."

Bimmy wondered how Hassan was going to react when the news of Pearla's murder came. "You decided what you gonna do wit' her?" he asked. "I mean, if you find out that she's fuckin' with that nigga Cash?"

Hassan lingered on his answer, staring out the window as Bimmy headed toward the highway. "What you think I should do with her?"

Bimmy felt it was a test. "At the very least, cut that bitch off, my nigga. Make her penniless. Pardon me for calling her a bitch, but you know what I mean. I got nothin' but love for you, Hassan, and I'm glad you home, because these streets weren't the same without you around."

Hassan nodded. "It's cool."

Bimmy was trying to be respectful and a real nigga all at once. If he played it too soft, there was a possibility that Hassan would catch on, and, if he went too hard, then Hassan might wonder why the sudden animosity. Bimmy had his own little chess match happening inside the Escalade.

Bimmy's cell phone rang again. He allowed the call to go through his Bluetooth and through the speakers in the truck. He wanted Hassan to listen in on this certain call.

"Yo, it's Bimmy. Speak to me."

Big Dee's raspy voice sounded through the speakers. "Bimmy, it's Big Dee. Yo, you alone?"

"Nah, nigga, I got Hassan wit' me."

"He home?" Big Dee asked in disbelief.

"Yeah, the nigga home. We ain't told anybody."

"Oh shit!"

"What the fuck, nigga? Talk to me!" Bimmy shouted.

"Yo, you ain't heard, Bimmy. Yo, I don't know how to tell you this. Shit, I hate to be the bearer of bad news . . ." Big Dee's voice trailed off in sadness.

Bimmy was growing impatient. "Nigga, stop fuckin' hesitatin' on what the fuck you gotta tell me. Just say it, nigga!"

"It's April."

"What about April?" Bimmy asked, his heart beating like drums in a rock concert.

"She's dead."

"What? Don't you mean Pearla?"

"Nah, it was April. They shot her, yo. Killed her in the Van Dyke Homes. Pearla is still wit' the body."

"What the fuck!"

"You need to get out here. It's crazy hectic right now."

Bimmy couldn't stop his tears from falling.

Hassan was completely astonished by the news himself. But he was asking himself, *Why did Bimmy think it was Pearla who had been killed?* He noticed his friend was becoming an emotional wreck. "Yo, you need me to drive?"

"Yo, I'm gonna kill these niggas!" he screamed at the top of his lungs.

# TWENTY-NINE

The stench of death permeated the air as April's body lay across the hard ground, covered with a white sheet. Cops had the entire area taped off and secured with yellow crime-scene tape, and marked and unmarked cop cars were scattered everywhere on the Brooklyn block.

A few detectives stood over the body, and some crouched lower toward the victim, taking in everything with their trained eyes. Who had killed her, and why? Was it a revenge murder? Drugs? Or a crime of passion?

A crime scene photographer took clear pictures of the body and the surrounding area. The looky-loos were everywhere, staring at another homicide committed in their neighborhood. To them, it was "another one bites the dust."

Several detectives combed the area to ask questions and find witnesses, but like in any ghetto, people rarely talked to the police. Mouths got really quiet when the NYPD came around. They didn't trust cops, and they were scared to get involved, especially once they knew identity of the deceased.

Pearla stood off to the side, still in complete shock that April was dead. She was scared to death. Detectives were in her face asking for a statement from her, but she didn't know what to say. Just like that, her world was collapsing around her.

"How long have you known the victim?" the tall, suited, pale-skinned detective asked her.

Pearla was in a trance. She heard the man speaking, but she couldn't hear one word he was saying to her, the image of April's brain's being blown out still etched in her mind.

"Can you tell us what happened?" he asked.

It was a horrible thing to witness, and Pearla was the girl who'd been through it all. But she would never forget this. What was going to happen next? What would Bimmy think? Would he blame her?

The detective continued asking her questions, but like everyone else, she shut down. She didn't want anything to do with the police. She knew nothing, and she saw nothing. She just wanted to go home.

A block away from the crime scene, Bimmy's black Escalade came to a screeching stop and he leaped from the vehicle and ran toward the scene with Hassan right behind him.

As he got closer to the scene, he saw April's body sprawled out on the concrete and covered with the white sheet, with dozens of people gawking at the body.

Bimmy flipped out. "Nooooo!" he screamed. He attempted to run to her, but several cops grabbed him and desperately tried to restrain him. But Bimmy wasn't going for it. He had to get to her. He had to see if it was her. He had to go and hold her in his arms.

The cops pushed him back and cursed at him. "Get the fuck back!"

And he cursed back, "Fuck you!"

Bimmy was raging out of control. The more they kept him away from April, the more insane he grew. Until, finally, he clenched his fist and took a swing at one of the cops trying to restrain him and sent him flying backwards with a painful jaw.

The other cops jumped on Bimmy. He fought back, swinging wildly at a half dozen of them. Anarchy rapidly ensued, with fists flying everywhere.

Next thing he knew, Bimmy was being tasered on the ground, causing him temporary paralysis.

Hassan stood in shock on the sidelines watching them beat down his friend. There was nothing he could do. He had just been released, and he wasn't about to get locked back up.

Bimmy was taken into custody, but the looky-loos, many of whom had recorded the incident on their camera phones, had witnessed the entire ordeal. They even chanted, "Worldstar! Worldstar!" in their cell phone footage.

Pearla couldn't believe her eyes. With so much happening in one day, she thought she was delusional. There was no way Hassan was home.

The two locked eyes. Hassan stood there, a few feet from her, looking expressionless. She ran toward him and leaped into his arms. She was so happy to see him, tears started to leak from her eyes. He welcomed her with open arms.

Pearla knew there was a reason why Hassan hadn't told her he was coming home. She figured that April wasn't the one that was supposed to be killed; those bullets were meant for her. The thought had her terrified.

"We need to go!" Hassan pulled her by the arm away from the chaos in the projects.

As they walked away from the area, Pearla pulled out her cell phone and subtly dropped it down a sewage drain while Hassan wasn't looking. She had too much incriminating evidence on there between her and Cash, and she didn't have the time to go through it to make sure that all texts and voice messages from him were deleted. So she thought it best to get rid of the phone entirely.

"Where you parked at?" Hassan asked. "And where are the keys?"

It was then that she realized that April had the car keys on her when she died. She had taken them out of the ignition without Pearla even noticing. Damn, her day kept getting worse.

"April has the car keys on her," she said.

"Fuck it! We'll take Bimmy's truck. He left the keys in the ignition."

The two walked toward the Escalade parked a block away. Hassan didn't care about the Benz at the moment. Most likely, he would have it towed back to the house when everything calmed down. He was mostly concerned with Pearla and wanted to take her somewhere safe.

Hassan knew Bimmy would be okay. The nigga had done jail before. And, April, his heart went out to her. For sure, someone was going to truly pay with their lives for her murder.

The ride back to their place was an awkward one at first. Pearla stared aimlessly out the passenger window thinking about April. Was it her fault that she was dead? Where had Hassan suddenly come from, and why was he home? Or more importantly, how did he come home when there was no bail set and he was looking at numerous felony indictments?

One thing for sure, the man knew how to work miracles. She could never underestimate him. Whatever knee-high shit he got himself into, he was able to pull himself out.

But she was worried. Did he have an agenda? Would it be something foul toward her for her affair with Cash, that is, if he knew or believed it? Or was he truly happy to see her?

Pearla thought long and hard. How should she play this—defense or offense? She decided to strike first and go with offense.

But Hassan started to speak first. Doing sixty on the Belt Parkway, he turned and looked at his favorite girl and said, "I fuckin' missed you so much!"

"I missed you too, baby." She smiled.

"I swear, if that was you"—He clenched his jaw, glaring straight ahead—"if anything had happened to you, I wouldn't know what I would do. I would go fuckin' crazy."

"I know, baby. Me too."

"What happened today?" he asked her. "How did you end up with April?"

Pearla sighed. "I went to see April because I was alone and needed someone to talk to. We went and ate at the River Café, we resolved our issues, and it was cool. She wanted to smoke, and her truck was low on gas, so we took my car to the Van Dyke Houses to get some weed from her cousin. I sat in the car and waited, and when she came back out"—Pearla felt herself about to get choked up, and the tears started to trickle from her eyes.

Hassan glanced at his woman becoming emotional. He placed his hand on her thigh. "Baby, I'm home now. Believe me, there's not a soul out there that's going to hurt you. I promise you that. You're safe, baby."

Somehow, in the bottom of his heart, Hassan knew that Pearla was the intended victim, not April. Was it a coincidence that April was killed on the same day of his release? He didn't think so. It was all planned deliberately. Whoever murdered April didn't know Pearla, or they weren't that familiar with her, so Hassan automatically ruled out Kwan and Cash. So who? It was an inside job—a gun for hire. He knew it. He felt it.

Pearla started to cry her eyes out. Her tears were real, but at the same time, she was concerned. She had to be a bitch and lie. With her eyes teary and red, she looked at Hassan worriedly and said to him, "Hassan, I need to tell you something."

"What is it?"

"I lied about why I went to see April," she said sheepishly.

"What you mean? Why?"

She huffed, "I went to talk to her about what was going on . . . about the tension between me and Bimmy."

"What tension between you and Bimmy? About what?" Hassan's eyes started to fire up, and his tone was becoming more and more gruff. He already knew that the news wasn't going to be good. He waited for it fretfully. He wanted to know what she was afraid to tell him. He was losing his patience.

She blurted out, "Bimmy came at me. He's been coming at me a lot lately. He wanted to fuck me while you were locked up."

Hassan shouted, "What the fuck you talkin' about, Pearla?"

"I didn't want to tell you, Hassan. I knew this would break your heart and things would become strained between everyone. I told April about it before, but that's the reason she started acting differently toward me. I just wanted to clear the air and let her know what her man was doing. I know he's your friend and y'all grew up together, but he don't want the best for you, baby. He's changed."

Hassan gritted his teeth and clutched the steering wheel so tight, he could've snapped it in two. He accelerated more. He swerved on the highway, almost hitting a car on his right.

Pearla shrieked. The last thing she needed today was an accident. "Baby, slow down," she said.

"Do Bimmy think he can walk in my shoes?"

Hassan thought back and started to put two and two together, and now it was all adding up. Of course, Bimmy wanted him to green-light the hit on Pearla before he came home so she wouldn't be alive to tell him what really happened.

Pearla knew that her lie had just spared her life, but unfortunately, it was going to take Bimmy's. But she didn't care; it was one of those incidents where it would be charged to the game. Bimmy should have minded his own business.

# THIRTY

Avery and Dalou were celebrating like it was New Year's Eve 1999. They did it! They killed that bitch, and now it was payday for them. That meant more drugs, more liquor, and more whores to play with. And for Avery, it meant that he had gained the respect of his cousin.

"Dey doubted us, Dalou, and now look at us. We gonna get our respect."

"Yes, sir! You killed dat bitch, nigga. Blew her brains all over da street." He laughed.

"It was easy, nigga."

"I bet it was. You called ya cousin yet?"

"I'm 'bout to."

"Call dat nigga and let's get this money. Fuck it! Ask dat nigga if he got any more work for us."

"See, ya a thinkin' man, my nigga. I ain't ready to go home yet either."

It was late in the evening, and the two men were back in their motel room. The smoking gun that had killed April was on the bed. They were getting high, getting live and loud, and enjoying life. Avery had no regret about taking a bitch's life. He couldn't wait to see Bimmy again.

He called his cousin's cell phone, but no answer. It went straight to his voice mail. For now, he and Dalou were patient. They expected Bimmy to keep his word and pay them the five thousand dollars owed to them.

\*

Hours passed, and still there was no sign of Bimmy. Avery had called and left him several messages, but still no call back or even a text message. It looked like he was being completely ignored. Both men wandered around the room becoming more and more impatient.

"You sure you callin' the right number?" Dalou asked.

"Nigga, yes!" Avery was becoming agitated.

"Then where is he?"

"I don't know, but he better call back soon and pay us our fuckin' money. We ain't kill dat bitch fo' half the price."

Avery didn't have an address for his cousin. He barely knew anything about him except that they were first cousins and supposed family. Back in the day, they used to hang together, but that was back in the day.

Dalou regularly stared out the window and frowned. There was no sign of Bimmy. No truck, nothing. The parking lot was just too quiet for him. He spun back around, glowering with distress. "Ya cousin better not be tryin' to duck out on us. I need dis money, man. I swear, he better not play us or he's a fuckin' dead man too."

Avery nodded, agreeing wholeheartedly with his friend. If his cousin tried to play them and disrespect them after they drove several states to do a murder for him, then they would kill him too.

\*

The night went on with both men plotting to rob Bimmy. They now believed that there was more money where the five grand came from. When Bimmy had come by before, both men had already peeped his jewelry, the truck, the clothing, everything. If he had ten grand to give away so easily, then the wealth he probably had stashed away in his home could be countless. They started to plot on Bimmy. They felt that a home invasion was necessary, and they would have to do the unthinkable, and kill Bimmy, because there was no way he would allow them to live after that.

Avery didn't care, though. He was desperate. He was hungry.

So the two men hatched a plan on how to rob and murder Bimmy and his whole crew. They figured that after—or if—Bimmy ever paid them the five grand owed, then they would start to do some recon on him, get as much information as possible. They would follow him home, or to his stash house, anywhere valuable and seize everything he owned. But for this, they needed some extra help from Decatur. To them, it was a genius plan, and with the right manpower, what could go wrong?

Avery got on the phone and made a call back to home. There were plenty of goons back South thirsty just like them, and they were willing to do anything for a come-up. He told his ragged crew that there was easy money in New York City. Men named Rag Tag, Saul, Bonz, and Billy Dee were on their way north to link up with Avery and Dalou.

Dalou rolled up another blunt, sparked it up, took a needed pull, sat on the edge of the bed and said, "Yo, I'm horny right now. Let's go to the strip club. Shit, how much dough we got left?"

Avery went into their stash and counted it up. "Fifteen hundred," he said.

"That's it?"

"Yeah, nigga, that's it!"

The two men had gone through nearly five thousand dollars cash in just a few short days. But the party needed to continue. Dalou was in the mood for some girls—or more like, some pussy. The two men smoked a phat blunt and then headed out to a strip club in Brooklyn where the girls got butt-naked, and, for the right amount of cash, anything else the customer wanted. That same night, they continued the party at the motel room, bringing back several strippers to fuck and suck them off while waiting on Bimmy.

# THIRTY-ONE

Cash sat parked outside the six-story tenement building in Elizabeth, New Jersey, squatted low in the old Chevy he was driving. He had a .9mm in his hand and was dressed in all black. It was dark out, and the block was silent and still. It was a working-class area where many folks retired early to get up early in the morning to go to work.

He peered up at the fifth-floor apartment window with a pair of small binoculars and saw the living room and kitchen lights were still on. She was moving back and forth between rooms. Doing what? He had no idea. She was definitely busy tonight. He took a pull from the cigarette and kept chill, but also remaining on high alert.

Cash felt he had one up on Sophie and Kwan. That day they were supposed to meet at the Starbucks, he'd followed them back into New Jersey. The stupid muthafuckas didn't know they had a tail on them. He could have been anyone. Either they were too stupid to care, or bold enough to think no one would dare follow them home, or come after them.

He had been scoping out the area for days, and on this particular night, she was alone. Kwan had left an hour earlier. He'd climbed into a Tahoe with some goons and drove off.

He felt salty about Sophie not letting his indiscretion with Pearla go. He was pissed that she lied to him and tried to set him up. Now he would talk to her on his terms. He would have the upper hand, and things weren't going to be pretty.

He took one last drag from the cigarette and flicked it out the window. He waited for the lights to go off. He wanted the place dark, so he could be in the shadows like a ghost. She wouldn't even see him coming.

Finally, when the lights to the apartment went off, he checked the clip to his .9mm, and it was fully loaded. He cocked it back, stuffed the gun into his waistband, and exited the car. He crept across the street and made his way into the tenement building, already knowing the building code. He took the elevator to the fifth floor.

This was what he did for a living, sneaking around and doing dirt in the dark. He was a thief and a killer on the side. He'd never wanted to hurt anyone in the beginning, but everyone pushed him too far. They underestimated him, and now it was time to show Kwan and Sophie how he was able to survive for so long. He wasn't just a pretty boy with a big dick. He was a street nigga too.

He crouched near the door and pulled out a pick and tension wrench. He used the devices to apply pressure to turn the lock cylinder. He worked his magic on the door for a few seconds, and *bingo!* he had access to the apartment. It was like stealing a car. The stupid bitch hadn't even put the bolt lock on her door. He slid inside smoothly. The place was dark and quiet. He casually made his way to the bedroom, knowing that's where she would be.

He found Sophie in the bedroom sleeping on her side, her back facing the door. She was sexily dressed and looking lovely. He stood over her with a foul look. His eyes burned into her sleeping soul. That bitch was misery. She'd betrayed him when she lied and tried to have him killed. Cash felt nothing for her or that baby inside of her. The bitch was poison.

Something came over him, a violent spirit, and the first blow came quickly and so hard, he almost broke her jaw.

"Wake up, bitch!" he shouted.

The punch startled her half to death. Sophie was wide-eyed when she saw Cash in her bedroom beating on her. But she wasn't a weak bitch who would lie there and take it. She leaped from the bed and tried to grab the .380 on her nightstand, but Cash grabbed the back of her nightgown and yanked her back.

Sophie released a guttural cry and turned around and swung her fist at him. He got hit in the face, but he didn't stumble. She swung wildly again and flesh met flesh, and Cash backhanded her. She went flying to the floor and crashed on her side, hollering.

Cash towered over her and growled, "You tried to set me up! I wanted to trust you!"

Sophie glared up at him with a bloody lip. "My fuckin' brother is goin' to kill you."

"Fuck you and him!"

She struggled to her feet, but Cash kicked her back down.

She shouted, "Nigga, what you gonna do? Try and beat your baby outta me?"

"If that's even my fuckin' seed, you lyin' bitch!"

Sophie frowned intensely. Her breathing was hard. She bit down on her bottom lip and charged at him like a bull, and the two of them started to tussle violently inside the bedroom, knocking over pieces of furniture.

She tried to kick Cash in his family jewels, but he wasn't having it. He punched her repeatedly in the face and then threw her to the floor again. This time she landed on her stomach. Sophie howled at the horror of having a miscarriage because of him.

"You need to stay down, bitch," he warned her.

Sophie clutched her stomach. She was seething with vengeance and knowing that she was fighting for her life and her baby. She stared in the eyes of her aggressor. "When I kill you, I'm gonna kill your bitch-ass father next," she shouted. "And then we gonna find your whore moms and kill dat bitch too!"

Cash lunged at her, but Sophie had a special treat waiting for him. When he got close, she swiftly smashed the lamp across his head, halting his attack. The lamp left a cut across his forehead. Cash hollered and fell momentarily.

Sophia leaped up and went for her gun across the room.

Cash knew he couldn't allow her to have the advantage. He snatched his gun from out his waistband just in time. When Sophie spun around, her hand around her .380, and took aim, Cash did too.

But only one shot went off—*Pop!*

After the big bang, there was a deathly silence. Cash stood tall while Sophie was lying across her bed, her hands coated in blood as she clutched the bullet hole in her neck, looking at Cash in utter shock. She was scared and she was wounded severely.

Cash walked closer to her. His eyes didn't shed his hatred for her. He looked at her coldly and said, "You shouldn't have betrayed me, Sophie."

She couldn't speak. She was dying. Cash only wanted to give her a beat-down. He didn't want to kill her. Or maybe he did. He didn't know what he wanted to do when he was in her bedroom. Something malicious quickly came over him and he acted out aggressively. Now the woman who was once fun and lively in his life was dying right in front of his eyes. There was nothing he could do for her. The damage was done.

What he could do was save himself from incarceration. He went around the bedroom wiping it down, and making sure he didn't leave any of his fingerprints. He took her gun and his, and before he made his exit, he looked over at Sophie one last time. She was finally dead. She'd died with her eyes open. He felt nothing. Her murder was personal. He could have called 911, but maybe she would have survived. Maybe. But what was done was done, no regret, no remorse.

Cash hurried away from the apartment and the tenement and leaped into his car and was ghost. With Sophie dead, it was definitely time for a dramatic change in his life and for him to leave town. But he didn't want to leave town alone. He had the means, so now he needed his family.

*** 

The very next day Cash headed to Brownsville, Brooklyn, which was daring, especially after what he'd done to Sophie, but he wanted to see his pops. He needed to have a heart-to-heart with Ray-Ray. Now was the time for them to push forward and have a new start someplace different.

Ray-Ray was at his usual spot, in front of the corner bodega and liquor store on Rockaway Avenue. It was a sunny fall day, and there was Ray-Ray, dancing the morning away in his tattered clothes.

Cash drove up in his gold Lexus and honked the horn. He caught Ray-Ray's attention. The man smiled like always when his son came to visit him.

With enthusiasm from top to bottom, he danced his way toward Cash's car and slid into the passenger seat. "Look at my handsome and beautiful boy. How's your day been, Cash?" he asked genuinely.

"Let's go for a ride, Pops."

"You gonna take me back to that restaurant and let me see that beautiful waitress again?"

"I got someplace better in mind, Pops."

"Better? Oh, okay. Let's go for a ride then, son."

Cash pulled off the block and made a right, going toward the Belt Parkway a few miles south. If things went as planned, he and his father would never see Brooklyn again. In the trunk of his car was a quarter of a million dollars and a few guns.

Kwan would be looking to retaliate after his sister's murder, and no one in Cash's family would be safe. Lucky for Cash, he didn't have much family. He had no kids, his mother was a wandering whore, and his father was a panhandling drug addict. But he had to protect the ones he loved.

Now, he had no idea where Momma Jones was. But she was a survivor too. His mother had never been a team player, so it was going to be hard to convince her to go with them.

Cash hurried toward the parkway. He glanced at his father. "Pops, what if I was to say let's get on the highway right now and disappear?"

Ray-Ray looked confused by his statement. "Disappear to where, son? My life is here."

"It doesn't have to be."

"You bringin' up leavin' New York again? Why?"

Cash didn't want to hide anything from his father. He hesitated for a moment, gazing out the windshield and looking somewhat edgy. "Because I care 'bout you, Pops, and I want you to be safe."

"I *am* safe," Ray-Ray said.

"No, you're not! Look, Pops, I'ma keep it real wit' you. I did something bad—really bad, and because of it, they might come after you just to get to me. And these people I have beef wit', believe me, they'll kill you and me without a second thought to it."

"Murder?"

Cash nodded.

Ray-Ray sighed. "Oh, Cash, what have you gotten yourself into?"

"Something that I can get myself out of. But I had no choice."

"And you think leavin' the city will help?"

"It's a start, Pops. I got a quarter of a million in the trunk and a full tank of gas. We can go anywhere—south, north, west—you pick." Cash was getting closer to the parkway. He wasn't about to take no from his father this time.

Ray-Ray sighed heavily. He sat quietly as Cash left Brownsville and headed toward Bedford-Stuyvesant, where they eventually stumbled upon

Momma Jones arguing with a couple of teenage girls over some bullshit. Her blond weave was twisted, her eyes were bloodshot, and she had a forty-ounce Colt 45 in her hand.

Cash and Ray-Ray hopped out the car and approached. Cash was momentarily embarrassed by her appearance. Her spaghetti strap T-shirt left her belly hanging out, her acid washed jeans was several sizes too large, falling off her ass and showing her ashy butt crack, and she had no shoes on her feet. Momma Jones could barely stand up straight, her equilibrium was off. Any second the young girls were about to beat her down.

"Bitch, you better go and wash ya dirty ass 'fore you get beat the fuck down!" one girl said. "I'm tired of ya fuckin' mouth!"

"Suck my pussy, bitch!" Momma Jones stuffed her hand down her pants and pulled it back out. "Niggas pay top dollar for dis ass!"

"Ewww!" the other girl hollered. "You's a stink bitch!"

Cash jogged up. "Yo, yo, yo, y'all need to chill wit' all that."

Momma Jones spun around and didn't recognize her own son. She licked her crusty lips and tried to adjust her clothing. "Twenty for a blowjob, baby. Fifty, you can put it in all holes."

Cash snatched her up by her collar and yelled, "Ma! It's me, Cash."

Momma Jones tried to recognize her son.

Meanwhile, the young girls couldn't be silenced.

"Oh my God! That's ya mother! Ew! She's a nasty ho!"

Cash needed to get off that hot block and escape. He was too busy dragging Momma Jones into the car to be distracted by the tweens, but Ray-Ray wasn't having it. He slapped the shit out of both girls before retreating into his son's vehicle.

Within seconds Momma Jones had passed out in the back seat. Between his parents' funk and the stress from his looming murder, he almost lost his mind. But he had to stay focused.

Ray-Ray noticed where Cash was driving, nearing the Belt Parkway. They saw the sign, Belt Parkway West, Verrazano Bridge. Cash went west, toward the bridge. Ray-Ray wished he hadn't gotten into the car. Now, there was no way Cash was letting him out. It felt like his own son was kidnapping him.

Ray-Ray thought about the life he was leaving behind. Or pretty much forced to leave behind. It wasn't much, but it was something to him. Like he'd told Cash before, he didn't know anyplace else. New York City had always been home.

"I'm gonna take good care of you, Pops. Believe me," Cash said to him, seeing the look on his face.

Ray-Ray didn't want to be taken care of. He was a man that always made his own way and his own dollar, even if he had to beg, plead, and entertain people for it.

"It's for your own good," Cash added. "And hers."

"This is kidnapping, son."

"This is saving your life and mines."

Ray-Ray stared out the window despondently. He slouched in the seat and sighed with regret. Where would they go from here? His life was never going to be the same again.

They headed toward South Carolina. It was time for Cash to start an entirely new chapter in his life. One with his past completely buried. And he wanted his parents to come along for the ride.

"She'll never stay," Ray-Ray remarked.

"Then we'll make her."

# THIRTY-TWO

Pearla woke up early in the morning to find Hassan gone. She wondered where he could have gone. She hadn't even heard him leave. Hassan was a private man who never had to explain himself to anyone.

She sighed and stretched out across her bed butt-naked and smiled, thinking about the night before when she and Hassan made hot, steamy passionate love for hours. Every minute of last night was an earth-shattering one. Her pussy was still throbbing.

Hassan had put that hard black dick down on her. He had spread her legs and entered her in the missionary position. Pearla released a loud grunt at the motion of his rotating hips, feeling his erection buried deep inside of her. He was inside of her so deep, they felt like one. She had left scratches across his back. Her hands started to tense into fists as her whole body went stiff as a board beneath a passionate lover.

From position to position, Hassan stayed deep inside her. They went from missionary to doggy-style then sideways. No matter what position they were in, Pearla would go as limp as a wet noodle when her man pistoned his hard dick in and out of her. It didn't take long for them to shake with orgasms that seemed to race through their entire bodies.

Round two was even more passionate, and rounds three and four were the knockout rounds. Every inch of Pearla had shuddered with delight. She had multiple orgasms and squirted like a fountain.

While nestled against her man, feeling the aftereffects of some great dick, she made up her mind to never cheat on Hassan again. There wasn't a better man out there for her, and she couldn't ask for anything more. He took care of her, financially and sexually.

With Hassan gone for the morning, Pearla removed herself from the bed and covered her nakedness with a terry cloth robe. She went into the bathroom to do her business and then went downstairs into the kitchen to make some breakfast for herself.

She needed a new cell phone, having tossed the old one down the sewer drain. There was too much damaging information on there. With the pressure off her and on Bimmy, she had slept like a baby last night. Now it felt like her life was back to normal.

No Cash, no Bimmy, and no drama!

***

Hassan sat shotgun in the black Range Rover with Big Dee and two of his soldiers. They were parked across the street from the 73rd Precinct on East New York Avenue. They waited patiently in the early morning and observed uniforms and detectives come and go from the building. But there was yet no sight of the man Hassan was looking for.

Bimmy was being released on a misdemeanor charge. He'd caught a break, but his biggest threat was outside of the precinct.

Hassan saw Gwap, a soldier in Bimmy's murderous crew, leaning against his silver BMW near the precinct and obviously waiting for Bimmy to walk out the building. He was Bimmy's ride somewhere. Hassan wanted to know where.

Everyone was excited and happy that the boss was home. Hassan had wanted his release to be simple and dull. He wasn't one for too much attention like parties and extravagant homecomings. However, the word was out on the streets that the boss was home now, though everyone had thought he was down for the count and looking at a lengthy sentence, if not life.

There were issues he had to deal with, and business to take care of. Rikers Island had taken up too much of his time, and there was no way he was going back to that jail. Those who hadn't been loyal to him while he was incarcerated would pay the ultimate price. But one thing at a time. He was strictly focused on Bimmy.

Savage, one of Hassan's most lethal goons, sat in the backseat rolling up a blunt. Nothing good ever came when he was around. He was pure hatred and destruction. It was rumored that he had full-blown AIDS and didn't care about his life or anyone else's. He was Hassan's coldhearted killer on a leash, and once Hassan unhooked him, all hell would break loose.

Hassan was quiet inside the Range Rover. He had a lot on his mind, especially Bimmy's betrayal and disrespect to his woman. He wondered what Bimmy was up to. Why didn't he call to ask Hassan to bail him out? All of Bimmy's actions were suspicious. Hassan was convinced that Bimmy didn't call because Pearla wasn't dead and was able to tell him what Bimmy didn't want him to know. It was all breaking Hassan's heart.

What kept playing over and over again in Hassan's mind was when Big Dee had called Bimmy to tell him about April's murder, and Bimmy responded, "You mean Pearla." Why would he mean Pearla unless Bimmy had it all set up that way? Thinking about that diabolical plot continued to infuriate Hassan to the point where he was ready to tear Bimmy apart with his bare hands.

For now, Hassan kept everyone in the dark, including Big Dee, who sat behind the wheel of the vehicle and had no idea what was going on. He wondered why they were spying on Gwap and Bimmy and why Savage was in the truck with them. Big Dee knew the only reason to have Savage come along was when you were trying to stir up hell on earth.

After half an hour of waiting outside the 73rd Precinct on the low, Hassan watched as Bimmy finally walked out the building behind his lawyer and greeted Gwap with dap and brotherly hug. Bimmy had a few words with his lawyer before they parted ways. Then he got inside the Beamer, and Gwap drove off.

Hassan instructed Big Dee to follow them.

**\*\*\***

Bimmy sat still and silent in the seat, scowling. Drowning in guilt and sorrow, he couldn't stop thinking about April. Her murder was on his hands. There was no way he could ever forgive himself for hiring two fools to do a man's job.

When he retrieved his cell phone from holdings, he saw that Avery had been blowing up his phone. These ignorant niggas wanted the rest of the payment when the mother of his kids was dead. He was ready to rip both men to shreds, shit down their throats, and piss on their fuckin' corpses. The fury and anger he felt was overwhelming.

He told Gwap to go to the motel in Canarsie. Gwap drove in that direction without any uncertainty or conversation. The look in Bimmy's eyes said it all. He knew who had killed April, and he was out for revenge.

Bimmy called Avery's cell phone, and after several rings, he picked up.

"Cuz, what's up?" Avery answered excitedly. "Where you at?"

"Where you at?" Bimmy asked casually.

"We at the motel. Ya comin' through, right? Ya know we did dat thing fo' you."

"I know. I'll be there in a few minutes. Y'all niggas just stay there and chill. I got y'all money."

"A'ight, dat's what up, cuz."

Bimmy hung up. The sound of Avery's voice sickened him. It made his stomach churn. There was no force on earth that was going to stop their murders. He said nothing while Gwap drove. He just wanted to hurry up and get there. End this shit!

Bimmy was so consumed with rage and extracting revenge, he was unaware that they were being followed.

Gwap parked his Beamer in the parking lot of the Motel 6 in Canarsie. He killed the ignition and pulled out two pistols from underneath his seat. He kept one and handed Bimmy the second gun, both guns fully loaded.

They climbed out of the car simultaneously. Their faces were expressionless. They were at the motel for one thing only.

Gwap followed Bimmy. Bimmy stood in front of the door with Gwap standing right behind him. He took a deep breath and knocked twice.

It didn't take long for Avery to open the door and allow them inside.

\*\*\*

Meanwhile, Hassan was watching it all go down from his parked position in the truck. He wondered who Bimmy was meeting inside the motel room.

\*\*\*

Bimmy looked around the messy room and saw two buck-naked whores lying on the bed looking like they'd just been turned out. The entire room smelled like ass and weed. He looked at his cousin and said to him, "Yo, tell them bitches to leave."

Avery didn't hesitate. He grabbed a bitch by her ankle and pulled her off the bed. "Ya heard what my cousin said—ya bitches get the fuck out!"

Dalou laughed. He sat by the table in the room and was rolling up a blunt.

"I thought we were goin' to smoke?" one of the girls said.

Avery shouted, "Nah, y'all got paid, so leave, bitch. Get the fuck out!"

They hurried to get dressed and were pushed outside the room.

Avery slammed the door behind them and laughed. He then looked at Bimmy and asked, "You got da rest of our money?"

Bimmy stared at them chillingly, while Gwap stood by the door, poised for any and everything.

For a brief moment, the room felt still and tense. Something was wrong. Avery could feel it, and definitely see it in Bimmy's eyes.

Then suddenly, Bimmy pulled out his gun and aimed it at Avery's head, and Gwap did the same, training his weapon on Dalou, catching both men completely caught off guard.

"Yo, cuz, Bimmy, what's up? What da fuck is dis?" Avery asked, looking speechless.

"You're a fuckin' idiot—that's what this is." Bimmy then fired and shot Avery in the head, and the body dropped right by his feet.

Gwap did the same, killing Dalou where he sat.

Bimmy and Gwap left the room, climbed into the Beamer, and left.

\*\*\*

Still parked nearby were Hassan and his soldiers. Big Dee was about to follow them, but Hassan had different plans. He wanted to see who or what was inside the motel room they'd just walked out of. Everyone climbed out of the Range and carefully made their way to the motel room. They knocked on the same door, their guns out and held low by their sides, just in case they had to start shooting. They had no idea what was behind the door. They continued to knock, still, no answer.

Hassan had Big Dee pay the Spanish clerk for the master key. Big Dee was very persuasive over the young girl.

They finally entered the room, and just as Hassan had suspected— murder. He had no idea who the two dead men were. But he was certain that it was Bimmy trying to cover his tracks. He rifled through their pockets. Just car keys and drug paraphernalia.

Before leaving, they wiped down everything they'd touched inside the room then walked to the parking lot with the car keys. There were several cars in the parking lot. One in particular caught Hassan's attention, the Ford Focus with Georgia plates. He walked toward the car and pushed the alarm button to the car, and the car lit up quickly.

"Bingo!"

The men went into the car and looked around. Hassan opened the glove compartment and found the proof he needed. He pulled out a picture of Pearla, an expired Georgia license belonging to Avery Williams, and a few more pieces of drug paraphernalia. No doubt he was family to Benjamin, AKA Bimmy Williams. It was done. Bimmy was a dead man walking.

Before leaving the motel, Hassan paid the clerk one thousand dollars to erase the surveillance footage.

# THIRTY-THREE

Surrounded by his crew of murderous thugs, Kwan stood outside his sister's building in the drizzling rain and watched the city morgue carry out Sophie's body in a black body bag on a long stretcher.

Someone had the nerve to violate him and his family. Not his baby sister! The only sister he had. She wasn't in the game. Everyone knew if anything happened to her, Kwan would be coming at them with full force, like a runaway locomotive. But someone didn't get the memo.

He was breathing hard and tight, his chest heaving up and down like a panic attack was about to come about. His fists were clenched, and his eyes looked like they were in flames. The depths of hell could be seen in his eyes.

He tried to hold back his tears. He couldn't cry for her out in the open. He couldn't show any weakness. He was around the wolves, but his snarl was the scariest.

He watched the morgue handle his sister's body with care. They lifted the stretcher and placed her into the back of a van and closed the doors.

The cops were everywhere asking questions and combing the apartment and the area for any trace of her killer, but no hard evidence was left behind, and there were no witnesses to the murder. Kwan didn't need the help of police. He had his own investigating crew on standby, and they were going to be a lot more effective than the police.

"They ain't had to do her like that," he spoke out randomly.

"We gonna get whoever did this, Kwan. Best believe that, my nigga," Leaky said with conviction.

Kwan fixed his eyes on the vehicle her body was in. He looked nowhere else. He was consumed with anger, rage, sadness, and revenge all at once.

The police and detectives knew about him and were wary of him being there. When two detectives walked over to talk to him, Kwan warned them that he wasn't in the mood to talk. In fact, his goons had set up a wall between the detectives and him. The cops would have to go through them before they started fucking with him. Kwan and his crew didn't give a fuck about their badges. He just wanted to grieve without being harassed. Then, when his grieving stopped, there was going to be hell to pay.

Kwan didn't know who murdered his sister. He had several enemies gunning for him, but he had a few suspects. Bimmy and Hassan were at the top of his shit list, and perhaps Cash. He felt that Cash didn't have the heart or the reach to get at Sophie, but he didn't rule out that possibility.

Kwan vowed that he was going to make each and every last one of them feel the same pain and hurt that he felt. He wanted their loved ones to suffer and be tortured. He wanted payback, and he wanted this all to happen before Sophie's body was in the ground.

He pivoted and walked back to the truck he came in, and his men followed. They drove off in despair.

What made it even worse was that she was pregnant. They took life from him and her. She was having a boy, and Kwan was having a nephew. Now, there was no one. Everyone was silent.

They drove back to Brooklyn. Kwan held a meeting in one of his places, and with over thirty people present, he put it out there—contracts on numerous heads. For their family members, it was five thousand a head, and for the top dogs like Hassan and Bimmy, fifty thousand a head.

For that bitch nigga Cash—fifteen thousand dollars, dead or alive. In fact, if they could bring Cash in alive, then that was twenty thousand dollars in a nigga's pockets.

Kwan had every goon, thug, or soldier that held an allegiance spread out, search, and destroy. They went looking for Cash's pops, but to no avail. They hadn't seen the dancing buffoon in days. They searched for Momma Jones, but there hadn't been any sign of her in weeks.

Hassan was a harder nut to crack. His parents were supposedly living in some lavish beach house in Jamaica, compliments of their son. Hassan didn't have any siblings or kids. So once again, Pearla was on the menu. Bimmy was an only child too, and both his parents were dead, and so was his baby mama April. So they went looking for his three children.

But Bimmy was three steps ahead of Kwan. He'd sent his kids off to Jamaica to stay with Hassan's parents until things cooled down and he could get his head right about April. He couldn't afford to lose the only family he had left. His children were Hassan's godchildren. So Bimmy knew that he or his parents would never harm them. He didn't want his kids at their mother's funeral because he felt it could traumatize them.

Day after day, Kwan's bloodthirsty goons kept coming up short about everyone's whereabouts. There was no one around. Brooklyn had become a ghost town. His enemies had hit the mattresses. Kwan was going berserk and wasn't thinking rationally. He just wanted justice for Sophie. He wanted to find a victim and fast.

Word got to him about Monique, April's mother, and he didn't hesitate crashing into her East New York brownstone and assaulting her. Kwan knew she wasn't valuable to anyone's criminal organization and that, besides April, no one else really cared for her. It was a waste of time, but still he wanted someone to die.

All morning, they beat and tortured Monique in her bedroom. Kwan tried to get her to talk, thinking she knew something about someone, but she cried out that she didn't know anything. Yet they continued to beat her, burning her with cigarettes and throwing buckets of cold water on her. In the end, Kwan killed her anyway. It gave him great pleasure to do it on the morning of her daughter's funeral.

\*\*\*

The bodies found at the Motel 6 in Canarsie didn't register on anyone's radar. There was an article about the murders of Avery and Dalou in several newspapers. The motel clerk remained silent when questioned by detectives, and without prints, witnesses, and the surveillance video, it was quickly becoming a cold case to the NYPD.

Several days after the murders, a carload of goons from the Dirty South arrived at the motel. It was the address Avery had given them. Rag Tag, Saul, Bonz, Billy Dee, and two others climbed out of the old used minivan and walked to the motel room. They were all ready to put their murder game down. Avery had promised them that there was gold at the end of the rainbow, and they'd come gunning for it. Their palms were itching for that paper.

The men had never been to New York, and the towering skyscrapers, the many bridges that connected into the city, the traffic, the people, and the life, took them aback. It was a busy place, and a far cry from their hometown.

Rag Tag knocked on the room door. No answer. He continued to knock, knowing Avery had to be inside. He was expecting them. Still, no one opened the door. Rag Tag looked back at the other and scratched his head. He looked at the piece of paper the information was written on. It was the right city, the right neighborhood, and definitely the right room. So where were Avery and Dalou?

Rag Tag said, "What da fuck!"

"Where are these niggas?" Billy Dee said.

The men turned around and went to the management office. Rag Tag tried to interrogate the skinny male clerk about Avery Williams, but the clerk told him that he and another man were found shot dead inside the room a few days earlier.

Rag Tag couldn't believe it. Avery and Dalou were dead? How did it happen? He scratched his head in wonderment. New York City done swallowed them up and spit them out dead.

Avery's Down South crew couldn't do anything but turn around and go back home. Broke. It was a long drive for nothing.

# THIRTY-FOUR

The overcast day seemed appropriate for a funeral. There was a great chance of heavy rain that afternoon. Hassan sat at the foot of his bed dressed in a dark suit and dark shades, preoccupied by everything that had been going on. He had his issues with Bimmy, but he had adored April and wasn't going to miss her funeral. He was going to be there while his best friend and right-hand man grieved.

He allowed Bimmy to cry on his shoulder, allowed his parents to take Bimmy's kids for a few weeks in Jamaica, and even allowed Pearla to cook him meals, though she was against it. It was all part of his plan—make Bimmy feel comfortable and keep him close.

Bimmy was beside himself with grief and blame. He couldn't eat, he couldn't sleep, and he couldn't think straight. Hassan was perpetually asking him questions, pretending to be by his friend's side and wanting to know who would kill April. Bimmy would lie and say Cash.

Hassan explained to him that yeah, Cash was a lot of things, but he wasn't built to walk up to April and blow her brains out in cold blood. Even if he did have the balls, why would he do it?

Hassan and Cash went back to elementary school days, and though Hassan hated him, Cash's heart didn't run that type of cold. Hassan knew the truth and was steadily fucking with Bimmy, just to see how far his friend would take it. When he wasn't blaming Cash, he blamed Kwan.

Bimmy poured his heart out to Hassan, and it was the first time ever he saw a thug like Bimmy cry. He missed April deeply and apologized to Hassan about his actions and negativity toward Pearla. Bimmy was in an emotional state, but Hassan knew the muthafucka was full of shit.

Pearla walked into the bedroom and took a seat on his lap. She wrapped her arms around him and snuggled against him. She could see he was thinking deeply about something, and she had an idea what it was. The grimy muthafucka was on both their minds.

"Are you okay?"

"I'm good," he replied softly.

She released a deep sigh. She knew Hassan was keeping Bimmy close while knowing about his betrayal. Bimmy wanted her dead, and she couldn't live with seeing the nigga every day knowing that he'd put out a contract on her head. Somehow, fate had kept her alive, and she was grateful. Karma was a bitch, but she had to play nice to the grimy nigga because Hassan asked her to. He was going through a lot, but what about her? She didn't give a damn about Bimmy. Pearla felt like she'd lost ten years of her life because of him. She'd thought that, by now, Bimmy would be dead, hacked to pieces and left in a shallow grave somewhere dark and dirty.

The morning was fading, and April's funeral service was approaching. Hassan had been to too many funerals in his lifetime, having lost a lot of friends. The streets never played nice. If you were weak, stupid, or got caught slipping or snitching, then most times a second chance was nonexistent. Brooklyn was a graveyard full of lost souls.

But Hassan had ended the lives of so many of those who went up against him. Being a shot-caller, he had made mothers, wives, girlfriends and sisters cry.

"You ready for today?" Pearla asked him.

"I'm always ready. It's just another funeral."

"She was a friend."

"In this game you gotta know how to separate friendship from business. You get too soft, these niggas will lick you up like ice cream. Death is death, Pearla. You gotta know that shit is always goin' to happen out here. People always gonna die. It's just part of the world I live in."

Hassan was preaching to the choir. Pearla already knew the world he was talking about. She was no silver-spoon, privileged bitch from the suburbs. She grew up with a rough and vile mother and had to fight and steal to get the finer things in life. She fought for her respect in a bad neighborhood, and she even had to fight in her own home.

Briefly, she thought about that day when she'd killed her best friend for having sex with Cash. It was a cold moment in her life, and one that she now regretted.

The couple exited the suburban home and climbed into the black stretch limousine, and Bimmy was right behind them.

Pearla was disgusted by his presence, but she sucked it up and simply wanted to go and show her respect at his baby mama's funeral. Though she hadn't known April for too long, she had become a good friend. She held her sharp tongue, swallowed her malevolent, vengeful spirit, and rode to Brooklyn in silence.

Today, April wasn't the only one being buried. Hassan and Bimmy's friendship had died too. Hassan was only prolonging the inevitable until the time was right.

The black limousine pulled up on Howard Avenue in Brooklyn to pick up Monique. Bimmy had been calling her phone all morning, but she wasn't answering. Bimmy and Hassan knew that Monique wouldn't miss her daughter's funeral for anything. The news of April's murder hit her like a ton of bricks. She'd cried and cried.

Monique had a tight relationship with her daughter, so it was going to be hard to live without her. April used to spoil her mother with whatever she needed. Clothes, cars, jewelry, exotic trips anywhere around the world, it was all paid for by April. The two were like sisters. Monique was a woman in her forties, vibrant and full of life, but the loss of her daughter tore her apart.

Bimmy called her phone for the umpteenth time this morning, but still no answer. "I'm gonna go see what's up wit' her," Bimmy said.

"You go do that," Hassan said. "We ain't got time to waste."

Bimmy stepped out of the limousine looking sharp and handsome in his black suit and white tie, his black alligator shoes shinier than a Marine's up for inspection. His Rolex watch sparkled brightly like the North Star, and the diamond stud earring in his ear was almost the size of a boulder.

He walked into the brownstone and went up to her floor. As he approached the apartment door, he noticed that it was ajar. Instantly, he knew something was wrong.

Cautiously, he entered the place and pulled out his gun. He could feel it already—the stillness around him. He looked around and noticed the disturbance in the living room that continued to the bedroom.

When he went into the bedroom, he was shocked to see Monique's naked, battered body tied to the bed. *Not today!* he thought to himself. "Shit!" he uttered in disbelief. He moved closer to the body and touched it to see if she had a pulse, but there wasn't one. The body was still warm, and rigor mortis hadn't settled into her muscles yet. He'd probably missed her attackers by minutes.

He pulled out his cell phone and called Hassan downstairs.

"What?" Hassan answered curtly.

"Yo, we got a situation up here."

"What's the situation?"

"She's fuckin' dead."

\*

Hassan, Pearla, and Bimmy stood over the body. Monique was lying face down, bound to the bed by her wrists and her ankles, and had bruises on her back, neck, and arms, and cigarette burns all over her body. Monique didn't deserve to die like this, especially on the day of her daughter's funeral.

It was Kwan; there was no doubt about it. They all knew it. Kwan had no moral compass. He was a ruthless and mindless thug who was hell-bent on causing murder and destruction and hunting down everyone he hated. He wanted to wear the crown. He wanted to become the king of New York.

"What we gonna do wit' her?" Bimmy asked.

Hassan was silent. He had to think. They still had a funeral to go to.

"The nigga is out of fuckin' control, Hassan," Bimmy growled. "He killed April, and now he kills her mother. We need to find this muthafucka!"

Pearla was teary-eyed in the bedroom. She had never met Monique, but April used to speak about her all the time. "Fuck it! Leave her here," Hassan said.

Pearla said, "Leave her like this?"

"What can we do for her now? She's gone, and we still have a funeral to attend. Did you forget?"

If they were to call the cops, it was inevitable that they would miss the funeral today. Hassan had paid for everything. He barely knew Monique, but he was saddened by her demise. He turned and started to leave.

At first, Pearla looked hesitant, but then she followed him.

Bimmy frowned and lingered in the bedroom for a short moment. He puffed out his frustration and was the last to leave the room.

***

Bimmy struggled to hold back his sorrow as he stood over the mahogany casket in the church. Still, his tears flowed gradually and silently down his stock-still face. He had made the fatal error of hiring inept goons from the South, and that resulted in his baby mama lying in a casket. He would never again see the warmth in her eyes, feel her embrace, or be surrounded by her love. He felt completely numb.

There were over hundred people at her funeral and more flowers surrounding her casket than at a Kardashian wedding. There was nobody dressed better at the funeral than April. She was dressed in a twenty-thousand-dollar vintage Versace gown, and her hair and makeup were impeccably done. She lay inside the casket, her hands folded over each other. She looked asleep, not dead. The mortician had done a wonderful job with the body.

Bimmy lingered over her casket. He clenched his fists and frowned with tears falling down his face. He wiped them away quickly, almost feeling ashamed that he was feeling and looking so weak. Although the men who'd done this to her were dead, it still didn't ease the pain.

Before long, there were speeches from many guests and a song sung by a childhood friend of April's. The heartfelt song brought on a fresh wave of tears from everyone.

Afterwards, there were words from the pastor as everyone sat still and saddened inside the crowded church. He first read a passage from the Bible, and then he gave the eulogy.

Hassan and Pearla had front row seats.

Pearla became emotional. She couldn't fight back her tears. They trickled down her cheeks like her face was a drizzly day. She had been there when April was killed. The whole ordeal was still playing like a movie inside of her head—the sound of the gunshots ringing out and the image of April falling. It was hard not to think that it could have been her.

She couldn't take it anymore. It was all too much for her. "Excuse me, I need to leave," she huffed at Hassan and immediately stood up, quickly moving down the aisle and separating herself from the sadness and the casket. She hurried out of the church and into the street. She took a deep breath, but suddenly burst out in more tears and grief. Her body felt like it was about to collapse on itself. She took a seat on the church stairs and continuously took deep breaths to calm herself.

Everywhere she turned, there was drama and murder. Every man she loved was always part of some kind of criminal or illicit activity. When had her life ever been normal? When was there ever a time when she didn't have to look over her shoulder?

Pearla had lost friends and family. She thought, *If that was me in that casket, then who would come to my funeral?* She had alienated herself from everyone. She only had Hassan, but what if something was to happen to him, then what? She had her insurance stashed away in a bank—a break-the-glass course of action, in-case-of-emergency account—but if she was to ever leave New York City, where would she go? Would she ever find love again if, God forbid, something terrible ever happened to Hassan?

She took a deep sigh and dried her tears.

***

The Evergreens Cemetery, 225 acres of rolling hills and gently sloping meadows in Brooklyn and Queens, was April's final resting place. Dozens of people gathered around the open burial site and watched through their teary eyes as her casket was gently lowered into the ground.

# THIRTY-FIVE

Kwan was out of control. His bloodthirsty appetite for revenge was spiraling into a murderous turmoil that had bodies dropping all over the city. He didn't care who he killed or where he killed them. Any association with his foes, and they were dead. He had become a maniac. Sophie's murder fueled the fire inside him even stronger, and it came bursting out onto the city streets like hot lava from an erupting volcano. His kills were brazen, guns blazing, bullets tearing into flesh and bones, and a body or bodies left in public for the city to clean up.

Two men connected to Hassan were shot in the head in a white Cadillac on Remsen Avenue. They were found slumped in the front seat. Two weeks later a couple was viciously gunned down in front of their home on Clarkson Avenue. Over a dozen bullets savagely chomped their bodies. The couples were once close friends to Bimmy and April.

But the murders that made the headlines and lit up the media like the Rockefeller Christmas tree was a cop and his entire family slaughtered in their Bensonhurst home on 71st Street. Sergeant Mark Dornier was a fifteen-year veteran on the police force. Some suspected that he was a dirty cop and had ties to Hassan, but it was never proven. His wife of twenty years and both his sons, ages sixteen and nineteen, were shot execution-style in their bedrooms. The horrific crime caught the attention of the police commissioner and the mayor and was plastered all over the evening news. The NYPD had declared war against the culprits responsible for the heinous crime.

Kwan was behind it all. He was getting Hassan's attention, but there were men in his crew who were having second thoughts about it all. They were all hardcore killers, but when you execute a cop and his family, there was no coming back. Kwan was becoming more and more paranoid. Those who spoke out against him were dealt with accordingly.

He climbed out of the Tahoe flanked by several armed men and walked into the small warehouse nestled in the industrial part of Brooklyn, near the Navy Yard. He was escorted inside and led to a back office, where a few more of his goons were watching over two men, each bound to a chair and stripped to their underwear. They had already been beaten, but the best was yet to come. Both men pleaded with Kwan, begging for their lives.

Word had gotten back to Kwan about the two stirring up tension inside his crew, wanting to revolt against him. They felt he was leading them all to their downfall. It was becoming them against the world, and the world was too big of a place for a Brooklyn crew to take on.

"Look, Kwan, whatever you heard, it ain't true!" one man shouted.

"How the fuck you know what I heard, *M*?"

"I'm sayin', Kwan, it's a lie!" the other man declared.

"Shut the fuck up!" Kwan shouted. "Y'all muthafuckas think I'm stupid?"

"Nah, man, we never thought that."

Kwan wasn't in the mood to talk. He'd come for one thing, and that was to set an example. He turned and nodded to one of his men, who handed him a wooden baseball bat. He stepped closer to the first man, *M*, clutched the bat tightly, lifted it into air, and cracked him over his head with it.

Blood spewed from *M*'s head as the bat crashed against his skull, and he screamed out in pain.

Kwan continued to hit him again and again. No part of *M*'s body was safe. Kwan broke bones in his hands, face, and arms. He broke his nose and eye socket. After repeated blows from the bat, *M*'s face started to look like chopped hamburger meat. Then it got to the point where he stopped moving and screaming. He had fallen to the floor, and his blood started to pool underneath his body.

Kwan started on the second man right away, savagely beating him with the baseball bat like he had *M*. He bashed the man's brains out of his head, caved the side of his face in, and broke limbs and bones.

To Kwan and his men, witnessing a vicious beating was like another day at the office, but the savagery of the attack almost made the hardest men turn their head and puke. When it was done, two bloody bodies were laid across the warehouse floor.

"Get rid of them." Kwan said.

"Cut 'em up?" a man asked.

"No, dump these bitches in the street somewhere in Brooklyn. Let muthafuckas know out there that I ain't scared to kill even my own."

The man nodded.

Kwan turned and walked away with his bloodstained hands and blood-splattered clothes. He got back into the Tahoe like nothing happened and even grinned at his actions, stating to himself, "Now that was fuckin' fun!"

\*\*\*

The sight of Brooklyn at night from a project rooftop was a thing of beauty. Standing above everything, Kwan had a little bit of solitude as he stood on the hard gravel smoking a cigarette. He was armed with two guns stuffed into his waistband.

He looked at his neighborhood with a vacant gaze. Since Sophie's murder, he had been on a violent crusade against everyone. It was like he was a demonic Rambo, tearing everything apart. His crazy violence against rival drug crews and the police had escalated into something even his own men couldn't understand. They were with him, but scared of him at the same time.

Kwan heard the police sirens blaring from a distance. The city was always alive with something—trouble, murder, and the wolves. All at once, it felt poetic to Kwan. Because of him, the city was on fire with pandemonium and the murder toll was rising. The NYPD was cracking heads and taking no prisoners. No one was getting any money in Brooklyn because of the war and the killings. Kwan had created a domino effect of destruction.

The metal door to the rooftop opened, and the moment he heard it, Kwan spun around and pointed his pistol at Leaky, who took a step back with his arms spread out, looking shocked that his friend had a firearm aimed at him.

"Yo, Yo, Kwan, it's me, my nigga. Damn! You need to chill. I just came up to see if you were cool."

Kwan lowered the gun and stuffed it back into his waistband.

Leaky was a crazy, foul-mouthed, murderous goon just like Kwan, but he too was wondering where Kwan was going with the war. Lately business had been slow. Cops had been raiding numerous drug locations and making hordes of arrests. It was getting so bad in the streets that roughnecks were scared to jaywalk for fear of being locked up.

"Yo, niggas ready for tomorrow night?" Kwan asked.

"Yeah, they ready."

Kwan nodded. He took one last drag from the cigarette and flicked it off the roof. He continued to gaze at an illuminated Brooklyn.

Leaky told him, "Yo, Kwan, no disrespect, but you sure about this shit? You know I'm a nigga that's been riding wit' you since day one, but what you talkin' 'bout, it's some really crazy shit."

"You scared, nigga?"

THE HOUSE THAT HUSTLE BUILT - PART THREE

"I'm just sayin'—"

"You just sayin' what, Leaky? You either wit' me or against me. Which one? Huh, muthafucka?"

Leaky tightened his face and held back his response. He shook his head. There was no reasoning with Kwan. He officially had completely lost his mind.

Kwan had several warrants for his arrest, and his way of dealing with the law was to shoot back. He wanted to start shooting cops and make a violent statement that he wasn't to be fucked with.

"I'm wit' you, my nigga," Leaky replied halfheartedly.

"Good. We do this shit tomorrow night. Cops fuck wit' us, then we fuck wit' them," he growled.

The plan was to kill a cop wherever they stood, either on patrol in their marked cars or on beat, and create panic throughout the NYPD. Brownsville was his battleground, the Van Dyke, Brownsville, and Howard Houses.

Next, he planned to take an army to Hassan's studio and try to blow his shit up. Snitches on the street were telling him things that he wanted to know.

Leaky turned and left Kwan on the rooftop grinning madly about his sinister plan.

# THIRTY-SIX

Charleston was the oldest city in South Carolina, but it was attractive with a lot of history. Cash stepped out onto the balcony of the hotel he was in and stared at the deep, blue ocean that stretched for miles in every direction. It had been a long drive from New York, but the view was worth it. It was a gorgeous day, and he was taking in the clean air.

He felt liberated. He felt like he could stand out on the balcony forever and stare hypnotically at God and man's creation combined, from the rich blue ocean to the colonial-looking real estate that surrounded him.

He lingered on the balcony for a moment and then turned and went back into the room. Momma Jones was almost comatose on the sofa, and Ray-Ray was peacefully asleep in his bed.

He walked over to his father and stirred him awake. "C'mon, Pop, wake up. It's a beautiful day outside, and we got a lot to do."

Ray-Ray groaned and grumbled himself awake. He turned and frowned at Cash. "What's so beautiful about it?"

"Pop, c'mon, don't be like that. You can look at this city."

"I don't wanna look at it."

Cash sighed. Ray-Ray was already missing home. But they didn't have a choice; New York was just too dangerous for them to stay.

Cash believed he'd made the right choice and picked the right city. It was far different from Brooklyn; everything about it was stunning. It had a unique culture with distinctive people. He knew he could get used to the mild winters.

Cash was ready to explore the city. He had a lot of money on him, and no one in Charleston knew who he was.

"Pop, c'mon. Let's go get some breakfast," he suggested.

Ray-Ray grumbled again.

Finally, he got out of bed and forced himself into the bathroom. He slammed the door behind him. "This city fuckin' sucks!"

"C'mon, Pop, just give it a chance. I know you gonna like it here. It's gonna be just you and me, like Thelma and Louise."

"Fuck them dusty, dyke bitches!"

"Damn, Pops! C'mon, don't be like this. What happened to that cheery attitude you had back in Brooklyn?"

He shouted through the door, "That's because I was back in Brooklyn!"

Cash sighed again. "You gonna like it here, Pops, because I like it here. Shit, you ain't gotta look over your shoulders, and you don't have to be anyone's jester because I'm gonna take care of us. I promise, Pops."

Cash smiled when he heard the shower come on. He stepped away from the bathroom door and turned on the television. News was on. They were talking about a cop's family being killed in Bensonhurst and the spike of murders and violent crimes in Brownsville. He knew it was Kwan's doing. The sadistic fuck had lost his mind.

Cash was grateful that he'd left the city in time. He no longer wanted any part of that life. Though he wasn't a saved or spiritual man, he simply wanted something different for himself and his pops. He thought about the people he'd lost over the years, friends mostly, and he knew that he was the lucky one. He had survived when others he had grown up with were either in jail or dead.

Briefly, he thought about Pearla and Sophie—one was dead, and the other, he knew he probably would never see again.

He stepped back out on the balcony and looked over the city again. Yeah, this was the life—nice weather, new faces, and an estimated nine hundred miles from New York. He could see himself becoming a Southerner.

Cash and Ray-Ray went out to get some good ol' home-cooked breakfast at a soul food spot called Mama Moe's on State Street, right near the historic Charleston City Market. After breakfast, they went to explore the City Market and took in other historical sites in the city.

Ray-Ray was looking fresh in new clothing and had a haircut and a shave. He looked like a brand-new man. And his grumpy demeanor had cooled down.

"Yeah, Pops, this gonna be us from now on, new people in a different city doing different things."

Cash was ready to go straight. He wanted to invest his money in a nightclub, or perhaps real estate or a restaurant. A lot of folks didn't know it, but back in the day, Ray-Ray was one helluva cook. Whatever it was that he was going to get into, Cash planned on taking his time and doing it right. He didn't want to get into any more drama. He just wanted to live normal for once, maybe buy a house and meet a nice girl, settle down, and have a family.

Father and son continued to talk and laugh as they explored Charleston. As they came out of the City Market on North Market Street, something immediately caught Cash's attention. A powder-blue 2015 Audi R8 came to a stop at a red light just a few feet from where he and Ray-Ray were standing. Seated behind the wheel was a long-black-haired beauty with the prettiest hazel eyes Cash had ever seen, and skin so smooth, it looked slippery.

The two of them locked eyes fleetingly. She smiled his way and then averted her attention from him. The woman and the car were both gorgeous. Cash was stuck on stupid for a moment. It took him back to a time when he'd had some of the wildest times with women and cars. His heart started to beat rapidly.

*Damn! It would be fun to have them both*, he thought.

# THIRTY-SEVEN

At the corner of Bergen Street and East New York Avenue, a marked police car sat in the middle of the night. The area was desolate, and the project buildings across the street were quiet. For a moment, it seemed like crime had taken the night off for the two officers who sat in the car talking about their relationships and sipping on cups of coffee. One was married, and the other was dating.

The police radio was crackling but only with minor incidents in the area—a 10-90 there and a 10-11 a few blocks away. Other squad cars answered the calls. Officer Holland, a black male with twenty years on the job, and Officer Horne, a white male with ten, were enjoying the quiet night in the Ville.

"So I take this chick out to Red Lobster the other night," Officer Horne said.

"Red Lobster. Wow! I see you went big with this one, huh?"

"Ha-ha, you got jokes. But, anyway, I'm at Red Lobster with this beautiful blonde-haired, blue-eyed woman, and she's stacked, Holland." Officer Horne raised his hands to his chest, shaking them up and down slightly. "We're having a nice conversation, eating dinner and this bitch just up and rips one right there."

"What? Rips one?"

"She farted right there!"

Officer Holland laughed. "You serious?"

"Yes! I mean, I didn't even see it coming. I don't think she even saw it coming."

Officer Holland continued to laugh as he sat behind the steering wheel with his cup of coffee. Horne had plenty of crazy dating stories. "So what you do?"

"I just sat there and closed my mouth. I didn't want the smell to get in. But, damn! It stank. I think I lost my appetite."

"Yeah, I would too."

"So I get over it, right. I put that shit behind me, and we get to talking again. I'm enjoying my lobster, and ten minutes later, she lets another one loose, this one louder than the last one. I couldn't believe it. I'm like, *What the fuck! Seriously?* Shit, even the waiter heard that one. And just like that, my Barbie beauty turned into this stank Jabba the Hutt."

"Yeah, but I bet you still fucked her, right?"

"What?"

"C'mon, Horne, how long we've been partners now? And when was the last time you turned down some pussy?"

Horne laughed. "Okay, I fucked her. You happy?"

"No, but I bet you were."

"That bitch had some kind of flatulence problem. I'm serious. She needs to get that shit checked out." He laughed. "But not everyone is happily married like you, partner. Honestly, I don't see how you do it, being with the same woman for ten years."

"Fifteen."

"Fifteen years! So let me ask you something."

"What?"

"In the fifteen years you've been married, have you not once slipped up and planted your 'mister happy' in someone else?"

"If you're trying to ask if I ever cheated on my wife, the answer is no."

"Seriously? Not once? Nothing!"

"I love my wife. She's beautiful," Holland said proudly.

"But I mean, not even a hand job, or did a bitch just kiss the tip of your shit?"

"You wouldn't understand the beauty of fidelity. Besides, with everything going on today with STDs, why would I leave something that is safe and I enjoy? I love my family, and I love my home."

"That's why they invented condoms, my friend. Latex—you can never go wrong with one of those."

Officer Holland chuckled. "You're completely hopeless, Horne."

"Hey, I'm just enjoying life."

"Well, don't burn your dick off by enjoying it too much."

"And that's why God invented penicillin."

"Yeah, you're definitely hopeless, Horne."

"Man, you know these females, they love themselves a man in uniform. Especially a cop's uniform."

"Did you take this job to protect and serve, or just to get laid?"

"Both, my friend. I'm having the best of both worlds." Officer Horne laughed.

As the two cops talked and laughed inside the police squad on the Brooklyn corner, a grave threat was creeping their way. His name was Demetrius. He was sixteen years old and strongly influenced by Kwan and the older heads he hung around.

In the dark, he nervously walked toward the cops' car with a loaded .45 in his hand. Kwan was paying him handsomely to kill cops in the Ville, filling the boy's head with "Black lives matter only if we start taking cop's lives," and other garbage to amp him up.

Demetrius edged closer to the car from the rear. He stayed hidden in the shadows dressed in all black, the large hoodie he wore pulled over his head. His palms were sweaty, and his heart continued to beat like it was about to rip from out of his chest. But he was still determined to go through with the execution.

He took a deep breath and glanced around his surroundings. It was now or never. He walked briskly toward the car and was able to see the cops' silhouette from the back windshield. He outstretched his arm with the .45 at the end of it and squeezed the trigger, and the gun exploded.

*Bam! Bam! Bam! Bam! Bam! Bam! Bam!*

The bullets tore into the cop car, shattering the back windshield and the side windows, and ripping into both cops in the front seat.

Demetrius moved closer to the car and continued pumping bullets into the cops' heads, knowing they were probably wearing Kevlar. When the firing stopped, both men were slumped in their seats.

Demetrius took off running in the opposite direction like a damn track star. Several blocks away from the shooting, he was smart enough to know to dump the gun into a sewage drain.

\*\*\*

About a mile away, a similar incident was about to take place. A beat cop was patrolling the hallways and stairway in public housing in the early morning. He was alone. He took the stairway down to the lobby, and as he was about to walk outside into the fall weather, two young masked gunmen ambushed him from behind. They pumped several shots into his back and skull, killing him instantly. They took off running and vanished in the air.

In one night, three cops were dead. Kwan felt supreme. If the NYPD fucked with him, then he was going to fuck them right back—no Vaseline.

Within the hour, a sea of blue came rushing to the aid of their fallen brethren, flooding Brownsville with cop cars, marked and unmarked, blaring police lights, and hordes of detectives at both shootings, from veterans to rookies. The shooting was so reckless and senseless, police captains in their white shirts and gold bars were heavy at both crime scenes, and the police commissioner and mayor were already addressing the media about the incidents.

Kwan stood on the rooftop of the Howard Houses project and watched his handiwork from up above. He enjoyed seeing the NYPD in disarray. He took even greater pleasure watching them drag the two bloody bodies of the fallen officers out of the squad car.

The look on every cop's face, to him, was fuckin' priceless.

"Fuckin' pigs!" He smirked and continued to watch the show.

# THIRTY-EIGHT

It was Armageddon everywhere, and Hassan's main priority was to protect Pearla from any harm. The shooting death of three officers in the Brooklyn area was plastered across every news channel in the area. He knew it was Kwan's doing. Hassan pegged him to be loco and an idiot. The man was so reckless, his lunatic actions started to trickle down on business, and no one was getting any money. Hassan's own loss of income was starting to reach in the hundreds of thousands. It was already bad, with the two drugs factions killing each other, but with three cops killed in a one-hour time frame, not to mention the cop and his family being killed in Bensonhurst, shit was about to get a whole lot worse.

Hassan had close to ten of his goons watching, protecting, and escorting Pearla at any given time. When she left home, they would surround her like she was the Catholic pope. Where she went, they went too. This heavy security for her was to go on until Hassan could find Kwan and kill him.

Kwan had become America's most wanted. Everyone was scared of him. But not Hassan or Bimmy. They were even more determined to go after him with everything they had.

Pearla sat at the foot of her bed lotioning her legs and watching the evening news on the fifty-inch flat-screen TV mounted on her bedroom wall. The killing of three cops was taking over the airwaves. She watched as the mayor and police commissioner stood next to each other behind the podium at an urgent press conference at One Police Plaza, both men voicing their frustration at the spike in murders, and the brazen murders of three cops in one night.

"This shit is getting ridiculous, baby!" Pearla exclaimed. "Y'all need to find that muthafucka Kwan and handle him. He's fuckin' everything up."

Hassan emerged from the master bathroom with his lower half wrapped in a blue towel. He glanced at the TV and then looked at Pearla. "We gonna find him."

"He scares me," Pearla said.

"Well, he don't scare me. He's just another fool living on borrowed time. That nigga's time will come. Believe me, baby."

"Three cops in one night." Pearla sighed heavily and shook her head.

"You need to turn that shit off, baby. You know there's nothing ever good coming from the news. That's the white's man media."

She did what he asked, and the flat-screen went black. Though the TV was off, clicking off their problems wasn't that easy.

Pearla stared up at her king, looking sexy in his bath towel. "What's the situation with Bimmy?"

"I know what you're thinking, and I didn't forget."

"I hope not. He got April killed because he wanted me dead. You can't never forget that, Hassan. You can't trust him."

"I know I can't."

"So why do you still keep him around?"

"Because I need him."

"Why?"

"Because right now he's the lesser evil. Do you fuckin' see what's goin' on out there? That muthafucka Kwan won't stop until we're dead or he is. I need Bimmy's skills on them streets to help hunt that lunatic down."

Pearla sighed deeply. "It's your call, baby. I believe in you. I just hope this plan of yours doesn't backfire on you. I love you too much to lose you."

"Baby, I'm not goin' anywhere, believe me. I'm here for you until we get old or a hundred, either one."

She smiled. "Well, I got your back too."

"I know you do."

They kissed passionately. Their tongues became entwined, and Pearla could feel the juices already building up in her pussy. She was ready to slide her hand up the towel and bring something to life between his legs. Every time their mouths touched, a jolt of electricity would pass through her, electrocuting her with lust.

He was her knight in shining armor, and when he finally got rid of Bimmy and Kwan, the two of them could finally live in peace. It was all she wanted, to live in peace and have a normal fucking life. She was tired of it all. There had been too much death and too many close calls for them both. It was time to get out. Pearla felt it in her bones.

"I want you out," she said to him out of the blue.

"What?"

"Get out the game. You can, Hassan. You have enough money saved and invested in legit businesses, including the record label you started, that you don't need the streets anymore. It's becoming too much."

He groaned. "You can leave the game, but the sometimes game won't leave you alone."

"Yes, it can and it will. Don't give me that excuse!"

"You want me to leave all this alone and go legit, huh?"

"Yes. We're getting older, and we need to become wiser, baby. How long before somebody gets the best of you and puts a bullet in your head? Or one day you can't get yourself out of jail? I want you with me, in my life, enjoying each other until we get old. Like you said, baby—you gonna be here for me until we get old or a hundred. I don't care which one."

"And what suddenly brought this on?"

Pearla stared off in the distance bareness for a brief moment before locking eyes with Hassan. "I'm pregnant!"

"Y-y-you're what?"

"I said I'm pregnant!"

"Seriously? You are? Oh shit!"

"Yes, you're gonna be a father, Hassan."

Hassan was over the moon about the news. "We gonna be parents. Damn!"

"I know, right?"

She and Hassan started to kiss fervently again. The news about the pregnancy made him extra horny.

He pushed her against the bed and made her spread her legs. Then he poised himself between her thighs and looked down at her. "You are the most beautiful woman in the world. And you're going to make a great mother."

Just as things were about to get really hot and heavy, Hassan's cell phone rang.

"Shit!"

"Baby, just don't answer it."

"I need to. It could be important." Hassan pulled himself away from Pearla and picked up his cell phone from the dresser, checking the caller ID. "It's Bimmy," he said.

She rolled her eyes. She was missing out on some dick because of him.

Hassan pressed the send button on his cell phone and answered, "What, nigga?"

"We hit gold," Bimmy said.

"What the fuck you talkin' about, Bimmy?"

"Kwan, that nigga's house is crumbling, and we gonna be there to pick up the pieces."

"Meaning?"

"One of his top goons reached out to me, some nigga name Leaky. He wanna talk."

"And you trust this nigga to meet?"

"Yeah, I do. This is our one chance to end this madness, Hassan. Let's hear him out."

Hassan thought about it for a moment. It could be a trap, but he felt he had to take the risk. He glanced at Pearla lying butt-naked on the satin sheets on the king-size bed. "Set it up then, and be smart about it, Bimmy."

"I will. Call you back wit' the details."

They ended their call.

Hassan stood by the foot of the bed looking pensive about the meet.

Pearla picked up on his sudden mood change. "What happened, baby?" she asked him.

"We might finally end this shit with Kwan."

"Seriously?"

He nodded.

"What's going to happen?" she asked.

He didn't want to tell her the details. It wasn't her business to know. He said, "I need some air."

Hassan donned a robe and stepped into the backyard for a cigarette and to think.

Bimmy called back with the details. "Tomorrow night, the boardwalk on Coney Island. He'll meet us there."

"A'ight."

\*\*\*

The black Range Rover came to a stop at the end of West 15th Street in Coney Island. Bimmy was the driver, Hassan rode shotgun, and two goons with assault rifles sat in the backseat. Straight ahead was the extensive wooden boardwalk. The chilly fall weather and the late hour made Coney Island a ghost town.

Hassan wasn't taking any chances. Meeting with one of Kwan's men was a risk. He may not be legit, and it might be a setup. Their Range Rover was the only vehicle around so far.

"Where is he?" Hassan asked.

"He should be here soon," Bimmy answered.

Hassan lit a cigarette and waited impatiently. He took a few pulls and said, "This better be for real, Bimmy."

"It is, trust me."

Hassan didn't any nigga who said, "Trust me." Bimmy was a snake in the grass. If Hassan didn't need him, Bimmy would have been had a large hole in his head. But Hassan had to be patient. He was going to use him until everything was taken care of.

A pair of bright headlights turned onto the street and slowly came their way. Hassan and Bimmy were fixated on the dark blue Infiniti Q50.

The car parallel-parked next to their Range, the headlights went out, and the doors swung open. Two men climbed out from the front seats.

Hassan watched them both carefully. He then uttered, "Let's do this!"

Leaky was average height, dark-skinned, and slim, wearing a do-rag and a long leather jacket. He had a serious look to him, and Hassan couldn't help but wonder how many of his men this wild-looking nigga had killed.

"You Leaky?" Hassan asked.

"Yeah," he replied casually. "I came in peace."

Quickly, both men sized each other up. They then decided to walk and talk on the boardwalk.

Bimmy wanted to follow behind, but Hassan instructed him to stay with the truck. He had this. Bimmy didn't like it, but he did what he was told.

THE HOUSE THAT HUSTLE BUILT – PART THREE

Leaky started with, "Look, that's my dude and I got love for him, but Kwan is losing his fuckin' mind. He's out of control. We ain't wit' that cowboy shit anymore—killing cops like that. It's always been bad for business."

"I agree," Hassan said. "So what you suggestin'?" Hassan didn't want to assume anything. He wanted to hear it from the horse's mouth itself.

"I'm sayin' he gotta go! He gonna bring us all down and get us fuckin' killed. I mean, I ain't no punk, but I got kids, my nigga. You feel me?"

"I do."

"And he on this warpath. I don't know what the fuck he's doin' most times. Since his sister got killed, he been trippin' and shit."

They continued to walk farther away from their cronies. Hassan was ready to find a solution to his problems tonight.

"What I'm sayin' to you is, I can give you the locations where he's gonna be, and you and your peoples can do the dirty work," Leaky said.

"And we will."

"And when he's dead, you and me, we can come to some kinda agreement on these streets. I know there's enough to eat for everyone. I'm just ready to start gettin' that money again. You feel me, my nigga?"

"Yeah, I feel you."

"Kwan got these cops so much up our asses, I can't even shit without feeling fuckin' brass. I just want it all to die down and go away."

"So how you wanna do this?"

"He trusts me, so I can bring him outta his hole and hand him to y'all easily. And then when he's gone, you and me can talk business."

"We can," Hassan said.

"So we cool?"

"We cool."

"A'ight, give me a week, and I'll serve the nigga up to y'all with no problem."

They shook hands then turned back around and began walking back to their men waiting calmly on the street.

Bimmy looked at Hassan wondering what had been said during their little walk. He anticipated that they had worked something out.

Hassan looked at his right-hand man and said nothing to him. He glanced at Leaky and said, "We'll talk."

Leaky nodded.

The men climbed back into their cars and went their separate ways.

Bimmy asked, "So what happened? He legit or what?"

"He legit."

"What I tell you? So Kwan's on his way out, right? I want that muthafucka, Hassan. Let me have him. I owe him plenty for what he did to my cousin Run-Run."

"In due time," Hassan replied matter-of-factly.

# THIRTY-NINE

Kwan stood over Sophie's grave in deep silence, feeling a bottomless pain in his heart. He stared at her headstone and frowned. He had sent his sister off right, sparing no expense, from the casket to her wardrobe. Sophie went out in style.

But he missed her so much. Rarely did people see a heartless thug like him cry, but standing over his sister's grave, he couldn't help shedding tear after tear. They had taken one of the best things in his life away. They had to pay. And he was making them pay severely, declaring an all-out war on everyone and becoming public enemy number one. He had set Brooklyn on fire. He had made the borough so hot, not even a blizzard could cool things off.

"I'm makin' these bitches pay, Sophie, for what they did to you. You were my little sister, and I loved you. I hardly told you that, but I'm tellin' it to you now," he said.

Kwan lingered by her grave wiping his tears. He knew who'd killed his pregnant sister in cold blood. He knew who was savvy enough to break into her home and murder her while she slept. It had to be Cash. He had the motive and the means.

The man was once his friend, but now Kwan had such a strong hatred for him that he placed a new contract of a hundred thousand dollars on his head. He'd hired two of the best killers to track Cash down wherever the nigga was hiding and kill him. Spiral and Lamont were the best at what they did. They were like bloodhounds when tracking down their victims and became pit bulls when tearing them apart.

As Kwan stood by his sister's grave, Leaky cautiously approached from behind, knowing Kwan was a jumpy nigga with a trigger finger. Startling Kwan could be dangerous to a man's health. So Leaky called out to him as he approached.

Kwan turned around, and all of his tears had been wiped away. "What the fuck you want, Leaky?"

"Good news, my nigga," Leaky started. He glanced down at Sophie's grave. "We all miss her, my nigga."

Kwan didn't care for his sentimental words, wanting Leaky to get to the point. "What you came here to say?"

"We found that nigga Cash."

Kwan couldn't believe his ears. "Where?"

"He fucked up. He's in the Bronx shacking up wit' some bitch," Leaky said.

Kwan hurried off with Leaky to the Bronx. He had such a hard-on for Cash, he instantly rushed to the first sighting of him, eager to tear him limb from limb. Finally, he felt he could avenge Sophie's murder.

***

The run-down house sat on a dead-end block in a neighborhood jumbled with mechanic shops, vacant lots, and garages on Bassett Avenue in the Bronx. It was only a stone's throw away from I-95, but he traffic on the freeway was light because of the midnight hour.

Bimmy came to a stop in front of the old home and shifted the Range Rover into park. He looked over at Hassan and said, "This is it, nigga—victory."

Hassan nodded.

They had gotten the call from Leaky an hour earlier informing them that they had Kwan in their possession. It was his gift to Hassan, as they planned on doing business together in the future.

Hassan was a little edgy as he, Bimmy, and three of their armed thugs stepped out of the Range and approached the house, where two of Leaky's men stood guard. With everything going down, he couldn't help but to think that there was no such thing as loyalty anymore. Leaky had betrayed Kwan—although for the greater good—and Bimmy had betrayed him.

He thought about Pearla. Had she ever betrayed him? Had she ever cheated on him? He erased Pearla from his mind momentarily. Right now, he had to focus and stay alert. He still had no idea what he was walking into.

Hassan and his men stepped into the house and were escorted down into the basement, where there was exposed plumbing, a century-old brick wall, concrete floors, and a single bare bulb dangling from the low ceiling. It was poorly lit and had a musty smell of cigarettes and mold.

In the center of it all was Kwan tied to a chair and surrounded by Leaky and his men. He was stripped butt-naked.

When Kwan saw Hassan and Bimmy enter the room, he shouted, "Y'all muthafuckas set me up!"

Bimmy smiled wide. He rubbed his hands together excitedly and couldn't wait to get at Kwan.

"You fucked up, Kwan," Leaky said. "We tired of your shit."

"Fuck you, Leaky! You gonna betray me for these fools? I'm gonna kill y'all niggas! I swear on my sister's grave, y'all are fuckin' dead! Dead!" He violently tried to twist around in his chair, but his restraints didn't budge.

"Yeah, nigga, I've been waitin' for this day for a while now," Bimmy said, walking closer to his prize, still rubbing his hands together. "You is fucked now, nigga!"

Everyone in the room was frowning intensely.

Kwan stared at his nemesis, and suddenly his tough demeanor changed. "C'mon, y'all, don't fuckin' do this to me! It ain't gotta be like this!" Kwan continued to plead. "We can make a deal. We can work somethin' out. How 'bout Cash, huh? I can get that nigga for y'all. Serve his triflin' ass up on a platter."

Leaky shook his head. The nigga was pathetic. His own men couldn't believe what they were seeing. The man could at least die in dignity and not beg. But he turned out to be a fuckin' coward. Leaky was glad to dispose of him.

Bimmy gripped the .40-cal. in his hand, his animosity transparent. The man's eyes glowed with resentment toward Kwan as he lifted the pistol to his head and uttered, "This is for my fuckin' cousin Run-Run, nigga!"

Kwan cried out, "Yo, please, c'mon, nigga. It ain't gotta go down like this. I'm sorry for what I did, yo. It was all part of the game, nigga. That's how it is. Nothin' personal, nigga, just business."

"Fuck you!"

*Bak! Bak! Bak! Bak! Bak!*

Bimmy put five shots into Kwan's head at point-blank range, killing him instantly. The force of the gunshots pushed him and the chair back, and the body fell to its side, thick, crimson blood pooling on the concrete floor. Bimmy exhaled, staring at his work. Finally! It was all over with. No more Kwan. Maybe now, things could get back to normal.

They planned on leaving the body on public display in the heart of Brooklyn, letting law enforcement know that the sadistic cop killer was dead and no longer a threat to them. As an added bonus, they planned on turning in the teenage shooters to the NYPD. They didn't want any more headaches with the cops.

Leaky stood over Kwan's body. He then looked at Hassan and asked, "So, we good now, right?"

"Yeah, we good," Hassan faintly replied.

"Damn! That felt good," Bimmy said, the smoking gun in his hand.

"Bimmy, get rid of that shit," Hassan said. "Let them deal wit' this clown nigga and the gun."

Bimmy nodded. "Yeah, you right."

Bimmy put the gun into Leaky's hand. The moment he surrendered the weapon, he found himself surrounded threateningly and being frowned upon, especially by Hassan. Suddenly he was the one in the hot seat.

"Yo, Hassan, what the fuck is this?" Bimmy asked.

"You already know, Bimmy," Hassan replied casually.

Bimmy smirked. He didn't need to be a rocket scientist to understand what was going on. He'd fucked up. His actions were coming back to bite him in the ass. He and Hassan locked eyes. Hassan held a .9mm. There was no escape from the inevitable. This was it.

"Yeah"—He chuckled slightly then said, "Just do it, muthafucka!"

Hassan elevated the gun to Bimmy's eye level and fired. *Boom! Boom! Boom! Boom! Boom!* He didn't stop until he'd emptied the entire clip into Bimmy's head and chest.

The man who was once his best friend, his right-hand man, was now lying face up and dead on the basement floor. Now he and Leaky had something in common.

Hassan felt no contrition—murder was murder, but this was payback. He was done. He was out.

Pearla was right—how long would it take before he saw himself on the other end of the barrel? He was ready to start a new chapter in his life. He was about to become a father, and he saw that there was no more loyalty in the game anymore. Everybody was turning out to be a snake, and there were too many snitches to count.

✳✳✳

Later that night, as Hassan lay in bed with Pearla, he told her that Bimmy and Kwan were finally dead. She breathed a sigh of relief.

The next morning, Pearla went into the bathroom to get ready for the day while Hassan was still asleep. She wanted to make him breakfast in bed. Cash was completely out of her system, and she was grateful to have gotten another chance with Hassan.

The thing that worried her was the paternity of her baby. She needed to do the math on the calendar, but first, she needed to find out how far along her pregnancy was.

She stared at herself in the mirror and placed her hand against her belly. It was still flat and sexy. She sighed. She was just hoping that when she went to see her doctor that the pregnancy time frame would accommodate Hassan.

She went back into the bedroom to find Hassan standing in front of the bed and grinning like a child. "What? Why are you smiling like that?" she asked, looking so happy.

"Because I love you."

"I love you too."

It was then that Hassan presented the black velvet box. Hassan crouched down on one knee in front of her and opened the case. Inside was the most gorgeous diamond engagement ring she ever seen.

Pearla's eyes and mouth opened wide with astonishment. "Oh my god!" she uttered.

"I want you to marry me," he said.

Pearla was in tears, and of course she answered, "Yes! Yes, I'll marry you!"

The following day, they went down to the justice of the peace and made it official. They were now a married couple.

That same week, they flew to Jamaica so she could meet his parents. They settled at his parents' lavish beachfront property in Montego Bay, the capital of St. James Parish on Jamaica's north coast. They explored Doctor's Cave Beach and Walter Fletcher Beach.

239

Pearla got to meet his folks, and they fell in love with her too. She was in paradise. Jamaica was a lovely, exquisite island. She didn't want to go back home. She had fallen in love with Hassan's family.

Although Bimmy had tried to have her killed, she had also fallen in love with April's kids. Both of their parents and grandmother were dead, so they had no legal guardian. Someone needed to look after them, and she didn't mind it. Once back in the States, she and Hassan planned on petitioning the court to become the legal guardians.

Pearla was about to have a family, and she was so happy.

# EPILOGUE

*Seven months later*

Hassan sat at his mahogany desk in his home office and watched Pearla and the kids splash around in the heated pool outside on a beautiful, fall day. Pearla's pregnancy was clearly showing as her belly protruded in her two-piece bathing suit. He smiled at his newfound family. He had completely left the game behind to focus on his record label, Heaven Records, and he had some talented rappers and singers on his roster. His company was blowing up legitimately.

He leaned back in his high-backed leather chair and thought over the choices he had made in his life, especially the one he made with Pearla.

His lawyer had come through with the paperwork for the kids, along with another envelope that Hassan had asked him for. He stared at the envelope and looked apprehensive about tearing it open and reading what was inside.

His lawyer, a trusted long-time confidant, saw the look on his face. "Listen, Hassan. I had my legal secretary compile the information, so I don't know what it contains. But maybe you should leave the past in the past."

Hassan sighed. He had never felt so nervous in his life.

"It's your call, Hassan. I'm simply the messenger," the lawyer said.

Hassan had asked his lawyer to retrieve all the text messages from Pearla's iPhone from the dates he was at Rikers. The information inside the envelope was either going to show that Pearla was true to him while he was locked up, or that she had been fucking Cash, or even Bimmy. He had a fleeting thought. *What if Bimmy was right, and everything that he told me was true? What if Pearla lied to me? What if Bimmy had a good reason to want her dead? And what if Bimmy was truly my only friend?*

These were very nerve-wracking thoughts for him. He loved Pearla and didn't want to read anything damaging inside that envelope. If everything was a lie, it would break his heart.

Hassan sat in his chair staring at the envelope and contemplating what he should do. He looked out the window again, and his eyes stayed on Pearla having fun with the kids. She was beautiful. She was all smiles. She had been good to him. She'd convinced him to leave the game behind, so they could start a family. But what was her truth?

Hassan lifted himself up from the chair with the envelope in his hand and tossed it into the fireplace. He groaned while watching it all burn. He decided to listen to his attorney and let the past be the past. He was a new man living a new life. Why take a sneak back?

Hassan managed to smile. It was time to grow, forgive, and move forward. Life was a series of choices, and he had made his. He chose Pearla. He chose to live happily with his new family in the house that hustle built.

# Don't Let the Dollface Fool You

# THE SERIES BY
# NISA SANTIAGO

And then, there's this

Book 5

Book 6